"Rafiq...I'm sorry for saying what I said before. I was angry and—"

"You needed to say those things, and I suppose I needed to hear them."

But he wasn't sure. She watched the firelight play on his taut features and enrich the dark olive tones of his skin. "Here," she said, and dipped a hand into the pocket of her jeans, then gently slotted a photograph into one of his hands. "I thought you might like to have this."

It was Robbie, looking all grown-up and smart in his school uniform, and wearing that familiar, rather sardonic half smile. It had occurred to her that Rafiq still had no conception of how like him her son was.

"It was taken in school only a few weeks ago," she explained. "He looks so like you that it came as a shock when I walked into your office this morning and realized…"

Her voice trailed away, dying on words that did not need saying, because she could tell from Rafiq's expression he was seeing … were fixed

D0967114

MICHELLE REID grew up on the southern edges of Manchester, England, the youngest in a family of five lively children. But now she lives in the beautiful county of Cheshire with her busy executive husband and two grown-up daughters. She loves reading, the ballet and playing tennis when she gets the chance. She hates cooking and cleaning, and despises ironing! Sleep she can do without, and she produces some of her best written work during the early hours of the morning.

If you've enjoyed *The Arabian Love-Child,* you have a chance to revisit San Estéban and enjoy the stories of Rafiq's friend Ethan, and his half brother, Sheikh Hassan.

Books by Michelle Reid

HARLEQUIN PRESENTS®
2254—THE SHEIKH'S CHOSEN WIFE
2272—ETHAN'S TEMPTRESS BRIDE

Don't miss any of our special offers. Write to us at the following address for information on our newest releases.

Harlequin Reader Service
U.S.: 3010 Walden Ave., P.O. Box 1325, Buffalo, NY 14269
Canadian: P.O. Box 609, Fort Erie, Ont. L2A 5X3

Michelle Reid

THE ARABIAN LOVE-CHILD

Hot-Blooded Husbands

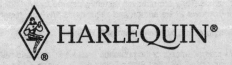

HARLEQUIN®

TORONTO • NEW YORK • LONDON
AMSTERDAM • PARIS • SYDNEY • HAMBURG
STOCKHOLM • ATHENS • TOKYO • MILAN • MADRID
PRAGUE • WARSAW • BUDAPEST • AUCKLAND

ISBN 0-373-12290-X

THE ARABIAN LOVE-CHILD

First North American Publication 2002.

Copyright © 2002 by Michelle Reid.

This edition published by arrangement with Harlequin Books S.A.

Visit us at www.eHarlequin.com

Printed in U.S.A.

CHAPTER ONE

RAFIQ AL-QADIM climbed out of the back of a chauffeur-driven limousine and strode through the plate-glass doors that guarded the International Bank of Rahman. In the clenched fist of one hand he held a rolled-up newspaper, in his eyes glowed a look that foretold of hell to pay for some poor fool. Hurrying behind him, his newly appointed aide, Kadir Al-Kadir, was wearing an expression that suggested he might be that very unfortunate person.

As Rafiq struck a direct line for the row of steel lifts set into a wall of grey marble, people in his path took one look at him and began backing away to give the big man an uninterrupted passage to his target. He didn't notice; he was too consumed by the blinding fury that carried his intimidating six-foot-four-inch frame into the nearest vacant lift. A dark-suited arm shot out; a decidedly murderous finger stabbed at the button for the top floor. The lift doors shut out Kadir Al-Kadir and the sea of stunned faces. No one who'd had any dealings with Rafiq Al-Qadim had ever seen him appear anything but formidably controlled.

But he was not in control. Rafiq had never been so angry. Rage was literally bouncing inside him, fighting to get out and vent itself. The lift took less than fifteen seconds to reach its destination. The doors opened; he strode out. Nadia, his secretary, took one look at his face, paled and shot to her feet.

'Good morning, sir,' she greeted warily. 'There have been several messages for you and your first appointment arrives in—'

'No calls. Nothing.' He cut right across her and kept on walking, each of his powerfully constructed, sleekly toned

5

muscles moving him with stallion-like grace to behind his office door, leaving Nadia staring after him in a state of near shock, for she too had never known Mr Rafiq to be anything but staunchly even-tempered and rigidly polite.

Rafiq's private office was a statement in architectural drama. High ceilings, marble floors, a window that was a wall of glass, in front of which a large slab of grey marble rested on legs of forged steel. As he moved across to it the pale sunlight of a London winter morning shot shards of cold steel through his black hair and added a sharpened cast to his lean dark profile that spoke of his ruthless Arab heritage.

Stepping around the edges of the slab of marble, he slammed the newspaper down on its smooth grey top. It unfurled on impact, showing him the inner-page headline that his aide had helpfully presented to him. It was Kadir's job to scour the world's newspapers, his job to mark those items he believed would be of interest to the acting head of the International Bank of Rahman. But Kadir would not be making the same mistake again very quickly, Rafiq mused as he glared at the reason for all of his anger. He had been duped, he'd been betrayed, he had been taken for a fool by a woman. And there it was, splashed all over the page of a Spanish tabloid: his private life uncovered, picked over and mocked at.

'SHOCK ANNOUNCEMENT,' block capitals proclaimed. 'SERENA CORDERO DROPS BILLIONAIRE SHEIKH TO MARRY HER DANCE PARTNER, CARLOS MONTEZ.'

His skin began prickling against his clothing, sharp white teeth setting behind the grim line of his mouth. Only two months ago she had been clinging to him like a limpet, adoring him, begging him, telling him she could never love anyone else.

The liar, the cheat, the unfaithful little slut. As far back as six months ago his brother Hassan had warned him about Serena and Carlos Montez. Rafiq had dismissed those rumours as mere publicity to add spice to the current world tour the two flamenco dancers were embarked upon. Now he knew the truth and he could taste the bitterness of his own conceit and arrogance at having believed that Serena could not have wanted another man while she could have had him. Only twice before in his life had he ever been betrayed by a woman: once by his mother, and once by the only woman he had ever let himself love. After that last bitter experience he had vowed he would never be betrayed like that again.

Yet here he stood, pulled into the betrayal trap by yet another woman, and he was so angry he could spit nails into the half-page picture of the beautiful Serena, smiling into her new husband's handsome face.

His mobile phone began to ring; dragging it out of his pocket he put it to his ear.

'*Querida*, please don't hang up. I need you to listen to me!'

His face, like his height and the tough, muscled build of his body, made no compromises at the best of times but the low dark sensual tones that hit his ear made his face take on properties as cold as the marble and steel that surrounded him.

'The tour is in trouble. We needed a sensation to put our names on people's lips. I love you, Rafiq. You know I do. But marriage between us was never a possibility. Can you not accept this situation for what it is?'

'You are someone else's wife. Do not call me again,' he incised, and broke the connection before tossing the phone from him as if it was contaminated.

Silence arrived, buzzing in his ears like a thousand wasp wings. In front of him lay the discarded phone and the damning newspaper. Behind him lay the rest of the world who would now be laughing at him. He was an Arab in every way you wished to look at him. Make an Arab look a fool and you win yourself a life-long enemy.

Eyes like black opals turned almost silver at the prospect. Picking up the newspaper, he flung it sideways and watched as it landed in the waste-paper bin. Serena Cordero's name would never reach his eyes again, he vowed as the other telephone sitting on his desk dared to start ringing. Black opals fired as a hand snaked down and long fingers closed round grey plastic as if it was someone's throat. 'I thought I said no calls!' he bit into the mouthpiece.

'By your tone I presume you have seen the news today,' a very dry voice drawled into his ear.

His half-brother, Hassan. He should have expected it. He swung himself down into his black leather desk chair. 'If you have called me to say I told you so, then take my advice and try silence,' Rafiq returned grimly.

'May I commiserate?' Hassan wryly suggested.

'You may mind your own business,' he snapped, then added tautly, 'Does our father know?'

'You think we swap gossip about your love life?'

'I don't have a love life,' Rafiq hit back with bite. This had been part of the problem with Serena. Finding a time when their busy schedules came to together had been almost impossible. If he had seen her twice in the last few months he could well be exaggerating, for while Serena had been travelling the world in one direction with her flamenco dance troupe he had been travelling in the other direction, attending to business duties that usually belonged to Hassan.

'How is Father?' he enquired as one thought led to another.

'He is well,' his brother assured him. 'His blood count is good and his spirit is high. Don't worry about him, Rafiq,' Hassan added gently. 'He means to meet his first grandchild, believe me.'

This time Rafiq's sigh was heavy. The last six months had been a trial for all of them. The old sheikh's illness had been long and miserable, spanning years of waste and pain. But six months ago it had almost taken him from them. With thanks to Allah, he had rallied on hearing the news about his coming grandchild. Now the disease was in remission, but no one could say how long it would remain that way. So it had been decided that from then on one of the two brothers must always be at home with their father. He needed the comfort of their presence. *They* needed to know that one of them would be there if his new-found strength should suddenly fade again. With Hassan's wife Leona in the latter stages of a much prayed for pregnancy, Hassan had elected to stay at home and deal with internal matters of state while Rafiq did all the travelling, taking care of the family's international business interests.

'And Leona?' he enquired next.

'Round,' her husband drawled satirically. But Rafiq could hear the pleasure there, the love and the pride. He wished he knew what those things felt like.

Then, he told himself forcefully, no, he was not going to go down that particularly rocky pathway, and turned the conversation to the less volatile subject of business. But when he rang off he continued to sit there seething and brooding and contrarily wondering why it was that he was so angry.

He had never loved Serena. She had been speaking the truth when she'd said marriage between them had never been a possibility. She was beautiful and hot—the perfect bed partner, in fact—but love had never been the engine that drove them through the passages of pleasure, even if she'd liked to use the word to him. It had been sex, good sex, but just sex for both of them. And sitting here wishing for love like his brother had was a damn fool's game.

But the small lecture brought him to his feet and sent him to stand staring out of the window. He was remembering a time when he had once thought he had found the kind of love Hassan was enjoying—had believed he held it in his hand like a precious diamond only to discover it was merely paste. Since then he had never looked for love;

he had no wish to feel its tortuous grip again, harboured no burning desire to pass on his genetic fingerprint. That delight belonged to Hassan and Leona, both of whom were worthy candidates to make the successful genetic mix. Whereas he…

That muscle within his chest called a heart gave a squeeze and he grimaced at the sensation. Alone. The sensation spoke to him of a bleak dark sense of aloneness that made him envy all of those people he could see moving about in the street below because they probably had good wholesome relationships to go home to at night, while he—

Well, he stood up here in his marble tower, personifying the rich and powerful and enviously privileged, when sometimes, like now, he felt as poor as any beggar you might pick out on any street corner—emotionally anyway.

Serena's fault? No, not Serena but that other woman, the one with hair with the same golden sheen he could see on the woman standing in the street below. Melanie had ruined him. With a calculation that belied her beauty, her shyness and innocence, she had taken a younger Rafiq, full of confidence and optimism, and had turned him into this hardened cynic he was today.

Where was she now? he found himself pondering sombrely. What had the last eight years done for Melanie? Did she ever think of him and what their affair had done to him? Or had she simply moved on, left him so far behind that she would struggle to remember his name if they had the misfortune to come up against each other again? He guessed the latter—he *knew* the latter. Melanie might have possessed the face of an angel but she owned the heart of a harlot. Harlots did not remember names; one merged in with the many.

Behind him his mobile phone burst into life again. It would be that other harlot, Serena, he decided. She was not the kind of woman to give up easily. Did he answer? Did he leave it? Had he dropped down so low in his own estimation that he was actually asking himself those questions? His teeth came together, gleaming white against the satin darkness of his olive-toned skin as he let the phone ring and glared down at the street where the woman with the golden hair was still hovering, as if she was unsure what she was doing or where she was going. He understood the feeling, could even sympathise with it.

In fact, the golden-haired stranger had more chance of getting him to answer her call than Serena did, was his final thought on the subject of female betrayal.

Standing on the pavement outside the imposing marble, glass and forged-steel frontage of the International Bank of Rahman, Melanie tried very hard to convince herself that she was doing the right thing by coming here. The building was big, and it was bold; it spoke of no compromises when she knew she desperately needed many compromises if her plan was to succeed.

Could it succeed? Was she wasting her time by coming here to see a man she knew from experience held no respect for her at all? Remember what he said, remember what he did, a small voice in her head cautioned. Turn around, Melanie, and walk away.

But walking away was the easy option. And easy options had never come to her. It was either do this or go home and tell Robbie nothing, she determined. And if those two options were not the same as being caught between a rock and a hard place, then she didn't know what was.

So, think of Robbie, she told herself firmly, and set her reluctant feet moving towards a giant pair of plate-glass doors reinforced by solid-steel tubing that defended the entrance to one of the most prestigious investment banks in the world. As she approached she glimpsed her own reflection in the polished glass doors and didn't much like what she saw: a too-slender woman with pale hair caught into a neat little topknot and an even paler complexion touched by strain. Her eyes looked too big, her mouth too vulnerable. Overall she looked just too darn fragile to be taking on an arrogant giant like Rafiq Al-Qadim. He'll step on you and not even notice, she warned her reflection. He'll do what he did to you the last time and freeze you out with his black opal stare.

No, he won't because you just won't let him, she told herself forcefully, and kept her feet moving as the pair of doors slid open with a stealthy silence that made her insides curl.

Like its exterior, the International Bank of Rahman's inside was a cavern of more glass, marble and steel. Glass walls for three floors gave her glimpses of open-plan office spaces flickering with busy computer screens and even busier people. Here in the foyer a marble fountain pushed moisture into the air while tall exotic plants tried and failed to soften the cold, cold atmosphere. People wearing statutory grey or black moved about with the confidence of those who knew exactly what they were doing here and where they were going.

It was sharp, it was sophisticated—it was everything she wasn't. A point that would have made her smile at any other time, because she knew who she was and she liked that person. The cut-throat world of high finance held no fascination for her. Never had, never would. But as she stood looking around she was forced to accept the grim truth that, hate all this though she might do, she had still dressed for the occasion in a sharp black suit that blended in perfectly here.

Deliberate? Yes, it had been deliberate. She answered her own question as her high-heeled shoes took her across the busy foyer towards the line of steel-faced lifts. She had dressed to impress, to make him stop and think twice before he tried throwing her out again. Melanie Leggett in jeans had never managed to do that, but Melanie Portreath in a designer suit might.

A stainless-steel plaque set between two of the lifts

listed the names of the departments and the floor on which
each was situated. She hovered for a moment or two, unsure as to which department she should be making for,
then realised that it could only be on the top floor, because
high-powered executives liked to keep their minions firmly
beneath them.

As she should know, having been there once upon a
long time ago. She'd played the worshipping minion to a
superior ego and had learned the hard way what it was like
be walked all over. It wasn't the best memory she could
have picked to take with her into the lift, Melanie realised
as her heart began to pump unevenly. Pressing the top-
floor button, she barely felt the lift move it was so efficient,
so nerves were putting that sinking feeling in her stomach,
she determined. Nerves and just the teeniest hint of excitement about what she was about to do.

Face the truth, an eight-year-old truth, a dark and po-
tentially dangerous truth. The lift doors opened, her knees
began to shake as she stepped out into yet another foyer;
this one was much smaller and bore the refined trappings
of luxury in the soft carpet covering the floor. A steel-
framed desk stood in front of a floor-to-ceiling stretch of
glass covered by vertical blinds. A dark-haired woman sat
working at the desk. She glanced up at Melanie's approach, came to her feet and smiled.

'Mrs Portreath? How nice to meet you.' Her voice, like
her smile, was warm and pleasant, the slight accent falling
in with her dark and gentle Arabian looks. Coming out
from behind her workstation, she presented Melanie with
a hand. 'My name is Nadia,' she announced. 'I am Mr
Al-Qadim's secretary. I am afraid Mr Al-Qadim is running
a little late this morning,' she went on apologetically. 'And
the information your lawyer sent ahead of you arrived on
my desk only five minutes ago. Please...' she indicated
towards several soft-leather chairs '...make yourself comfortable while I check if Mr Al-Qadim is ready for you.'

Not for me, he isn't, Melanie thought as she watched

Nadia walk towards another giant pair of doors, made of solid wood this time. The secretary paused, seeming to need a moment to gather herself before she knocked rather tentatively on the door, opened it, stepped through and closed it behind her.

That small hesitation left Melanie standing there having to deal with the next rush of uncertainty that attacked her resolve. Rafiq was on the other side of that door, and if his secretary had to steel herself to go anywhere near him then what chance did she have of meeting a sane and sensible man?

Arrogance; she was suddenly remembering the hardened arrogance that could add such cold condemnation to his lean face. He was a man who could freeze out the world by just standing in silence, a man who could shatter a person with just two small words: 'Get out.'

Her stomach muscles collapsed on the crippling memory. In the space of six short weeks he had wooed her into loving him. He had asked her to marry him and promised her the earth. He had told her that no one could ever love her as much as he did, then he had taken her to bed and wooed her of her innocence. Then, on the evidence of one cleverly constructed scene, he had simply turned his back on her with those now immortal words, 'Get out,' and had never looked at her again.

Did she really want to subject herself to that kind of humiliation again? she asked herself. Was she crazy to risk exposing Robbie to the same?

The urge to change her mind and just walk away while she still had the chance rose up to grab at her again; panic of the sort she hadn't experienced in a long time actually set her feet swivelling towards escape.

The door behind her opened. 'Mrs Portreath?' his secretary's smooth voice prompted.

Melanie froze—utterly. She couldn't move, not a muscle; she couldn't even bring herself to draw in breath. It was awful. For a horrible moment she wondered if she was going to faint.

'Mrs Portreath…?'

Remember why you are doing this, she tried telling herself. Think of Robbie. He loves you and he's suffering right now, feeling the vulnerability of his own mortality and, more significantly, yours. Rafiq does not know what he turned his back on eight years ago. He deserves this chance to know about Robbie, just as Robbie deserves this chance to know him.

But she was scared of what it was going to mean to all of them. Rafiq was from a different race and culture. He viewed things through different eyes than she did. He might not want to know about Robbie. He might fling this chance right back at her and…

'Mrs Portreath? Mr Al-Qadim will see you now.'

Mr Al-Qadim will see you, she repeated anxiously. Did it matter if he did toss Robbie aside? It would be his loss if he did. Robbie never needed to know about this visit, but if you'd asked him outright, he would say it was worth any risk. So do this one small thing for him and you might start to sleep nights.

Small. She almost laughed, because this was no small thing. It was huge, colossal, as big and unpredictable as the big man himself.

'Get out' her head echoed. What did those two cold words do but expose a man who was unwilling to face up to *his* responsibilities? Let him use them again, she decided as her chin lifted. She could take the rejection for Robbie. She had done it before, after all. Her conscience could be cleared and she could then walk away to get on with the rest of her life, and more importantly Robbie's life, knowing she had at least tried.

'Yes, thank you,' she heard herself murmur, and by the time she turned to face Rafiq's secretary she was back in control again, with her eyes clear and her slender shoulders set into a determined line. One of the doors to the office stood open. Nadia stood to one side of it, waiting for Melanie to step by. With only the smallest increase in her pulse-rate she walked towards that open doorway and through it, with her smile fixed and ready to meet fate full-on.

The room was just another play on steel and marble. It was huge, with high ceilings and wall-to-wall glass that framed a desk built of marble and steel. In front of the desk and standing slightly side-on stood Rafiq Al-Qadim. He was wearing a dark grey suit and was leaning over slightly with one big hand braced on the desk while he read the set of papers in front of him.

Her papers, Melanie recognised. Her requirements. Her nerves began to flutter. Had he seen? Did he know yet? A clammy sweat broke out on her skin as she stood just inside the door and waited for him to lift and turn his dark head so she could make that first stunning impact on eyes that, even after eight long years, still visited her in her dreams.

Rafiq was being deliberately slow in straightening to acknowledge Mrs Portreath. He was wishing he hadn't agreed to this meeting. The woman might have inherited the Portreath fortune, but even her healthy millions were small fry to an investment bank like this. Randal Soames, the executor of the Portreath estate, had talked him into this interview. He was doing it as a favour to Randal because the woman herself was being so stubborn about wanting to use the services of the bank and, more significantly, she had insisted on seeing Rafiq. In his mind, if she'd managed to get the hard-edged Randal Soames to go against his own better judgement it made her one very manipulative woman.

He despised that kind of woman. Was learning to despise the whole female sex with each betrayal they hung upon him. If he had a choice he would have them all locked up in harems to use only when necessary. They called them the weaker sex, the vulnerable sex, when really they were stronger and more dangerous than a whole army of men.

'Mrs Portreath to see you, sir,' Nadia prompted. It was a brave thing to do when his secretary was already aware that his mood was about as volatile as an active volcano.

But it also meant that he had taken too long to lift up his head. So, gritting his teeth together behind the flat-lined set of his lips, he attempted to put some semblance of a smile on them as he straightened up and made himself turn to face the woman he was already predisposed to dislike.

What he found himself looking at shut his heart down. What he saw standing not fifteen feet away made him have to wonder if he was actually losing his mind. He could not believe it. He had conjured her up. Any second now two more women were going to walk through the door and stand right beside her: Serena and his mother. The three witches.

As that dark head lifted Melanie felt her breath begin to feather, felt her pulse begin to accelerate. He hadn't changed, was her first breathtaking observation. He still had the build of a Roman gladiator and a proud cut to his jaw line that warned of no weakness anywhere. His hair was still as black as midnight, his hands as big and strong as she remembered them to be. He could fill a room like this with his size and the sheer electrifying force of his presence.

Yet his height and his size and his deep inner reserve had somehow always made her be very gentle with him. Why was that? Melanie asked herself now as she stood facing her past with the puzzled mind of maturity. It wasn't as if he was a vulnerable giant. If anything, he had been cruel and heartless, utterly ruthless in his method of discarding her.

Her eyes took their time lifting to clash with his eyes. She was expecting to be frozen by cold disdain but what she found herself dealing with shook her to the core. For she was looking at Robbie's eyes, Robbie's beautiful, al-

most black eyes that were looking back at her with the
same sensational long eyelashes that could turn her insides
to soft, loving butter. And Robbie's wonderful high slashing cheekbones, Robbie's perfectly, perfectly moulded
mouth.

And the beauty, dear God, she'd forgotten the masculine
beauty in those lean dark high-born features that could flip
her heart over and set her senses singing to the kind of
tune she'd experienced with no other man. It hurt, oh, it
hurt, because she was standing here staring love in the face
again.

How could she not love, when she was seeing the man
who had shaped her son's image? she thought despair-
ingly. It was like looking into the future and seeing her
beloved Robbie as he would be thirty years on: the height,
the riveting dark features destined to breaks hearts just as
his father's had done. Did that forecast worry her, or did
it touch to life maternal pride, knowing she was in the
process of rearing a heartbreaker for a son? She didn't
know, couldn't think, didn't even know why she was ram-
bling over such ridiculous things when there were far more
important issues to consider.

But her insides were a mass of shakes and tremors, her
eyes stinging with the onset of tears. Tears for a lost love,
a broken and irreparable love. She didn't want to feel like
this; she hurt as badly as if it was only yesterday that he'd
thrown her out of his life.

A movement behind her caught her attention. Rafiq's
secretary was hovering, probably wondering what was going on. Neither she nor Rafiq had moved or even spoken.
Rafiq was frozen, his face held by a shock so profound it
was clear that he was in no fit state to say a word.

Which left that mammoth task to her, Melanie realised.
She'd planned this moment, spent hours rehearsing it in
her head. All she had to do was find the strength and the
will to put her plan into action. But it wasn't easy. She
had come here believing that Rafiq had killed everything

she used to feel for him. Now she knew that wasn't the case, she accepted, as she set her feet moving across a vast space of marble until she came to a stop just an arm's reach away from him.

She looked up—had to—he was six feet four inches, a towering figure in comparison to her five feet eight. It wasn't a bad height for a woman, but compared to Rafiq she felt like a pocket miniature. He had shoulders that were three times the size of her slender ones, hands that could easily span her waist. His torso was lean and cased in hard muscle, and his legs—

No, stop it, she told herself fiercely as things began to stir inside that she just did not want to feel. She lifted her eyes, made contact with the dark, dark disturbing density of his still shocked eyes that seemed to want to pull her like a magnet into taking another step closer.

She resisted the urge, held it back with a fist-grabbing catch of control. Then, with every bit of sophistication she had acquired over the past eight years, she murmured, 'Hello, Rafiq,' and even managed to hold out a surprisingly steady hand. 'It's been a long time, hasn't it?'

CHAPTER TWO

IT CAME as a punch to his stomach. The truth—reality. Melanie was standing here in front of him. No ghost, no spectre dragged up from the depths of his own bitter memory. The same spun-golden hair, darker gold eyes, creamy smooth skin covering perfect features; the same small, soft kiss-needy mouth and that soft-toned sensually pitched voice which brushed across his senses like a long-remembered lover's caress.

Yet in other ways it was not the same Melanie. The clothes didn't match, nor the way she styled her hair. The old Melanie had worn jeans and battered old trainers, not handmade leather shoes with spindles for heels and a slender black suit that shrieked the name of its designer label. Her hair used to stream around her face and shoulders, freely and simply like a child's, though then she had been a twenty-year-old woman.

'What are you doing here?' he rasped out without any attempt to hide his contempt.

'You're surprised.' She offered a wry smile. 'Maybe I should have prewarned you.'

The smile hit his system like burning poison, seared through his bloodstream on a path that had no right to gather in his loins. He shifted, ignored the hand. 'You would not have got beyond the ground-floor foyer,' he responded with a gritty truth that sent her hand sinking to her side.

It also wiped the smile from her face, and with it Rafiq felt the heat in his body begin to dissipate. She shifted uncomfortably—so did someone else. Dragging his eyes across his office, he saw his secretary standing by the door.

Fresh anger surged, a burning sense of bloody frustration, because this was the second time today that Nadia had witnessed him behaving like an ill-mannered boor.

'Thank you, Nadia.' He dismissed her with icy precision.

His secretary left in a hurry. Melanie turned to watch her go. Give it an hour and the whole building was going to know that Mr Rafiq was undergoing a drastic change in personality, he was thinking grimly as Melanie turned back to face him.

'She's afraid of you,' she dared to remark.

'The word you mean to use is respect,' he corrected. 'But, in truth, your opinion of my staff does not interest me. I prefer to know how you dare to think you can safely walk in here masquerading as someone you most definitely are not.'

Eyes that reflected the winter pale sunlight streaming in through the window, widened. 'Oh, I'm sorry, Rafiq. I thought you knew who I was. Didn't you receive the papers from my lawyer's office?'

Since those very papers were lying on his desk in front of both of them, it was sarcasm at its infuriating best. But it also made its point. Rafiq's eyes narrowed. 'You mean you actually are the Melanie Portreath who inherited the Portreath fortune?' he demanded in disbelief.

'Don't sound so shocked,' Melanie responded dryly. 'Even poor little country girls can have a lucky change in fortune occasionally.'

'Marry it, you mean.'

The moment he'd said it Rafiq could have bitten his tongue off. It was hard and it was bitter and gave the impression that he might actually still care that she'd been seduced by his wealth.

'If you say so,' she murmured, and turned away to take an interest in her surroundings. As she did so he caught the delicate shape of her profile and felt something painful tug at his chest. Damn it, he thought. Don't do that to me.

'This place is as cold as a mausoleum,' she told him.

She was right, and it was. Leona was always telling him the same thing. His half-brother Hassan's office, which was next door to this one, had received a full makeover by Leona's gifted hand to make it more hospitable. But Rafiq refused to let her anywhere near his office because— because he liked mausoleums, having placed his life in one, he accepted with an inner sigh.

Maybe Melanie knew what he was thinking, because she turned suddenly and their eyes clashed again, golden light touching bleak darkness, and the years were falling away. She had once told him that he was incapable of feeling anything deeply, that his big test in life was to learn to trust his own feelings instead of deferring those judgements to others. 'You'll end up a cold and lonely cynic, Rafiq,' she'd predicted. 'Living on the fringes of real life.'

'What do you want, Melanie?' he demanded grimly.

'To sit down would be nice.'

'You will not be stopping long enough to warrant it.'

'It would be to your loss.'

'The door is over there,' he drawled coldly. 'My secretary will see you out.'

'Oh, don't be so arrogant.' She frowned at him. 'You could at least have the decency to hear what I have to say.'

'You can have nothing to say that I wish to listen to.' With that he turned and walked around his desk.

'Now you sound pompous.'

He swung on her so angrily that she took a shaky step back from the desk in alarm. 'I sound like a *cheated* man!'

The words rang in the space between them. Melanie looked into his face and felt her knees start to fail. Bold slashing features cast in bronze seemed to loom ever closer. Eyes spiked with bitterness threatened to shrivel her where she stood. His mouth was no longer a mouth, but a pair of parted lines between which a set of white teeth glinted with danger. And the cold slab of marble lying between them seemed to be the only thing holding him back from stretching out a large hand and taking hold of her by the scruff of her neck.

She was shocked. Oh, not because of the pulsing threat itself, but because she would never have believed that he could reveal so much of what was raging inside him. The man she'd used to know had been so fiercely controlled that it had taken him weeks to get around to admitting he was attracted to her. He'd used to haunt her family's farm on the pretext that he was considering investing money into it. He'd used to turn up in strange places like the tack room at the stables, or the hay barn, and would stand watching as she heaved bales of hay onto a low-loader ready for transport to the animals scattered about the outlying fields.

'You should not be doing this,' he'd said in husky disapproval.

'Why?' She remembered laughing at him. 'Because I'm a woman?'

'No.' He hadn't smiled back. 'Because you hate it.'

It had been a truth that had confounded her, because she hadn't realised her dislike had showed. She'd been living on the farm since she was ten year's old, had been expected to do her share of the many daily chores. But as for enjoying the life? No. She would have given anything to go back to how things used to be, when she'd lived in London with two loving parents instead of one bad-tempered uncle and his weak stepson.

'You cheated yourself,' she now returned unsteadily. 'And you have no idea how badly you—'

'Quit,' he warned thinly, 'while you still can.'

It was an outright threat. Instinct was telling her to heed it, but anger was already welling up from the dark pit where she'd stored it for the past eight long years.

'As you did when you preferred to believe lies about me, rather than give me a single minute to explain what you saw?' she flashed back at him. 'Is this my cue to come over all tomb-like and walk out of here, Rafiq? Will it make you feel better if I leave you alone with your righteous belief that you were the only one injured eight years ago?'

'Get out,' he incised.

And there they were. Those magic words, delivered with the same black-toned lack of emotion as before, that literally froze her blood. Melanie looked into the cold dark cast of his face and thought, Ten minutes. It had taken just ten short minutes for them to reach the same point where they had finished things eight years ago.

She laughed, though it was a shaky sound, and swung away, aware that she might have mocked herself about those two small words earlier, but they were still having that same crippling effect on her now as they'd had then.

Only there was a difference. The younger Melanie had run; this older version was made of stronger stuff. She swung back, faced him squarely. 'I have something important to tell you first,' she announced.

'I have no wish to hear it.'

'You might regret saying that.'

'Leave, Melanie,' he reiterated.

'Not until you hear me out.'

Where had that damn stubbornness come from? Rafiq glared at her with a mix of frustration and fascination. It had been a hard push to get the old Melanie to argue about anything. Now he could not shut her up!

The telephone on his desk began to ring, and glad of the diversion he picked it up. It was Nadia informing him that his next appointment had just cancelled. 'Thank you,' he murmured, and returned the receiver to its rest, then glanced at Melanie. 'I'm sorry but my next appointment has arrived,' he lied. 'Which means that your time is up.'

Melanie stared at him. He could have done without seeing the hurt glinting in her eyes. 'You never intended to give me a chance, did you?' she gasped.

'Even as Mrs Portreath?' He arched a cold black eyebrow. 'No,' he confessed. 'I have a congenital dislike of machinating women, you see, so using Randal Soames to get you into this room earned you no more extra time than if you had managed to get in here as Melanie Leggett.'

And that, Melanie realised, more or less said it. She had failed in her mission even before she'd arrived here. What a joke, what a sad little joke. For a few moments longer she continued to stand there, looking at this tall dark beautiful man with the romantic face of Arabia and eyes fit to turn a desert to ice, and seeing no sign at all that there was anything worth appealing to beyond those eyes she knew she was going to give up the fight.

'You know what I think, Rafiq?' she said quietly. 'I think you've just lost the only chance you will ever be given to turn yourself into a human being.'

And with that she turned to walk away. From his chance, from Robbie's chance. The threat of tears suddenly overtook her, because she knew deep down inside she was walking away from her own last chance to make this man understand the truth about her.

I was a fool for thinking I could do it, she railed at herself. Rafiq needed a heart before he could care enough to want to listen. Robbie didn't need a man without a heart cluttering up his life. He had already known the best. It would be an insult to William Portreath's memory to now offer her son the worst.

'Wait…'

Her hand had a grip on the door handle. Melanie froze like a statue with her eyes to the door. What next? What now? she wondered tensely. Did she even want to hear it?

Yet she didn't move. Bigger fool that she was, she just stood there and waited, with her teeth clenched tightly and her heart pumping heavily, while behind her there was… nothing. He didn't speak again, nor move, as far as she could tell. And where the silence before had held a smothering sense of failure, this silence screamed with hope. Weak and pathetic, pained and helpless—hope.

She was trembling; Rafiq could see it happening. So

much so that the knot of silk hair was threatening to come loose. Was she close to tears also? He had a suspicion that she was—just as he had a suspicion that he'd just made the biggest mistake of his life by stopping her from leaving here.

But her last remark had got to him; it had touched a raw nerve inside that went back eight years to when he'd regretted not listening to what she'd had to say. The human being part had pricked him, because if anyone knew he was only half-human then it had to be himself. But here stood the woman he blamed for that.

So why *had* he stopped her when she could have been gone by now? Confusion at his own actions set him frowning as he threw himself down into his chair and tried to decide what do next. As he did so his eyes fell on the stack of papers he'd only had time to glance at before Melanie had walked into the room.

'Tell me about William Portreath,' he invited.

Her shoulders sagged a little, her chin dipping towards her chest to expose the long slender length of her nape. A nape he could almost feel against his fingers—fingers that actually stretched out on cold smooth marble in a featherlike caress. He drew them into a fist, sat outwardly relaxed in his chair while inside every muscle he owned had knotted in an effort to cast out what had been daring to take a grip. His gaze dropped to where her hand still grasped the door handle. Like him, she was dubious about continuing this.

The tension rose along with the silence, and his heart began to pump unevenly in his chest. When his mobile phone began to ring he was so glad of the diversion that he answered it without even thinking about it.

It was Serena again. Of course it was Serena. She had just remembered who was financing her tour, and was using her most seductive voice to try and make him see sense.

At last Melanie moved. He didn't. In fact his eyes, ears,

his capacity to breathe had all been lost in a stress-loaded moment as he watched her fingers slacken and finally drop away from the handle altogether. She began to turn. It was slow and uncertain. She began walking back across the room with her eyes carefully lowered so he could not see what was going on behind them.

Serena was turning on the heat now, the fact that he hadn't cut the connection giving her encouragement. She wanted them to carry on as they had been. She wanted him to remember what it had been like for them.

But *he* was remembering what it had been like with Melanie. He watched her come towards him in her smart suit that skimmed her slender body like a smooth outer skin, but he saw tight faded jeans and a simple tee shirt, saw himself peeling both from her wonderful flesh with hands that worshipped what they found. He saw beautifully formed breasts with rose-tinted areolae and perfect nipples that tightened at the slightest caress. His eyelashes grew heavy as his gaze skimmed downwards to recall the flatness of her silk-smooth stomach with its perfect oval for a navel and gently rounded hips that loved to be cradled in his. Shy Melanie, virginal Melanie, with a soft mouth that had trembled because she had wanted him so badly, and eyes glowing like topaz, aroused and ready to offer him her one precious gift. If everything else she had ever offered him had been lies then he knew without question that wanting him so badly she had had to give him her virginity had been Melanie's one truth.

Should that count for something now? he pondered grimly. In his own country it would count for everything. They would have been man and wife on the strength of that one night alone. Indeed, his sense of honour had already made that decision before he had claimed his exquisite prize. It was a prize that still held a power over him as he sat here in the present listening to one woman beg for his passion while the other aroused him without having to try. He recalled a single afternoon spent upon

an old-fashioned feather mattress beneath an eiderdown
when her arms had clung to him and her body had accepted him with small soft gasps that had rolled his heart
around. He had felt the barrier, could still feel it tempting
the proud crown of his sex. 'Yes,' she had said in that soft
breathy whisper, and it had stirred him beyond anything
he could ever remember.

He was in agony, he noted ruefully. But while he sat
here struggling with his own discomfort, he also had the
satisfaction of seeing Melanie's cheeks grow warm and her
eyelashes flicker in a way that placed a wry smile on his
lips. She knew what he was thinking and was unable to
look at him because she was feeling the effects of those
memories just as strongly as he was.

It was sex, nothing more. He could deal with sex—as
the beautiful Serena would agree.

If he didn't stop undressing her with his eyes she would
change her mind and leave, Melanie decided as she sank
down into the chair by the desk. He was daring to sit there
looking as laid back as a man could look while listening
to a telephone conversation, but his hooded eyes were
burning through her clothing. Did he think she was too
dense to know what he was doing?

A wry smile twitched his mouth. It was a mouth that
should have looked mean and cold, but by some quirk of
fate looked anything but. She sighed, dropped her eyes
away from him and wished his expression did not reminded her of sex. One man, one afternoon, only that one
experience to call upon—and she was certainly able to call
upon it, she noted helplessly. All it had taken was a knowing glint in those eyes and she could see the man in all
his naked glory. The breadth of his wide bronzed shoulders
and long muscular torso peppered with soft dark hair
and—no, stop right there.

Who was on the other end of the phone that could hold
him in silence for so long? she wondered as she shifted

restlessly on the chair. She wished he would speak, if only to break this terrible tension that was eddying in the air.

Sexual tension. The man had always had the power to turn her inside out with that heavy-lashed, steady stare. Perhaps he knew it, perhaps the call had finished ages ago but he was stretching out the silence on purpose just to extend the agony. Could he be that calculating?

Yes, she decided, of course he could. He had made it very clear that he didn't want her here, but then for some baffling reason had decided to give her a chance to say what she'd come to say. Perhaps she'd touched a nerve when she'd challenged his status as a human being, and this was his idea of payback. Rafiq had pride enough for ten men. He had an ego as big as…other parts.

Oh, stop it! she railed at herself as a second wave of heat crawled up her cheeks.

Rafiq saw the blush and was reminded of the first time he'd seen her, at a friend's country estate. He had been there as a weekend guest and Melanie had been one of the paid staff. She'd served him throughout dinner, quiet, shy, and wearing a perpetual blush to her cheeks. Every time she'd leant over his shoulder to serve him he'd inhaled the scent of her delicate perfume, had felt the soft brush of her breath and her silk hair brushing his cheek. Electric, clinging… He stopped breathing for a moment in dark recollection. Twice she'd caught his shoulder with a serving dish and had almost died with embarrassment. Twice he'd found himself making a joke about his own size in an attempt to deflect the wrath of his hostess.

'She's new—temporary,' Sally Maitland had explained with the condescending tone of someone who had lived her whole life being served only by the best. 'Leave it, Melanie!' she had snapped in annoyance while Melanie valiantly tried to remove spilled sauce from where it had landed on the tablecloth by Rafiq's plate. Her hand had been trembling, the heat from her cheeks hot enough to heat his own cheek as she leant across him. 'You just can't get the staff these days. Melanie is more used to feeding chickens than people.'

He smiled at the memory, though it was more like a grimace. Melanie had fed him a lot that weekend. She'd fed his mind and his senses by being everywhere he'd happened to be. Her perfume had lingered in his bedroom whenever he'd walked back into it after she'd been there tidying the bed; her shyly lowered eyes had followed him whenever she'd had the misfortune to be serving food. If they'd met on the stairs she'd blush like mad and scurry hastily away from him; if they'd brushed arms or shoulders she'd jump like a startled kitten and refuse, though he'd tried, to utter a single word to him. Nods and shakes had been all he'd got for his trouble.

Nods and shakes that had almost driven him out of his mind.

'Come on, *querida*. Forgive me and let us put this behind us. Carlos is not expecting fidelity from me and I—'

With a flick of the hand he cut the connection. Melanie lifted her face. 'You didn't speak a single word,' she said, almost accusingly.

'No words were required,' he drawled lazily, and smiled the kind of smile that made her feel threatened and edgy and eager to get out of here.

'About William,' she said firmly, 'I think I should start by—'

'Lunch,' he inserted.

'Lunch?' Melanie offered him a perfectly blank stare.

He offered a smile to her. 'I think we will take this conversation away from the business environment and place it in a more…congenial setting.'

'But you have another appointment waiting outside!'

His answer to that was to reach out and pick up the other phone. Several smooth words spoken in Arabic and as far as Melanie was concerned the problem of his next appointment had been consigned to the archives. The phone went back on its rest.

'Problem solved,' he murmured with lying smoothness.

'I really do prefer to deal with this right here.' It was almost a desperate little plea.

'Oh, come.' He stood up. 'Here I am attempting to show you my human side by offering to listen to you, and you throw this gesture back in my face?'

If he thought listening to her talk over lunch was going to be pleasant then he was in for a surprise, Melanie thought ruefully. And why did she feel as if she'd just come face to face with a slippery snake?

She watched him warily as he walked around the marble slab. The dig about his human side hadn't passed her by either, nor the fact that in the space of a one-way conversation with his mobile phone his whole manner towards her had taken a complete reversal. He arrived at the side of her chair. The hairs on the back of her neck began to stand on end. He was waiting for her to give in and stand up, but her eyes were level with a certain part of his anatomy and what she could see happening there sent a wave of shocked heat sweeping down her front.

This had nothing to do with lunch, or talking, or even him showing his human side! It was to do with sex. Let-me-rumble-you-on-the-nearest-bed kind of sex—for old times' sake.

'Stop this, Rafiq,' she uttered tensely.

'Stop what?'

'You *know* what!' Jumping up, she took an anxious step back. The chair was in the way, the marble desk blocking any other form of escape. 'Let me pass,' she insisted.

'Of course.' He took a step sideways.

Flustered beyond daring to think, Melanie went to slither between him and the desk. His hand snaked out, caught her by the waist to bring her to a standstill. It was the first time he'd touched her in eight long years and it turned her senses into live wires that forced her to draw in a sharp breath.

He laughed huskily. 'Sure you want to go?'

She lifted her face to spit out her answer at him. Eyes clashed with eyes, hot and elemental. She parted her lips on a shivering gasp. Rafiq dipped his dark head and covered them. She fell into his kiss like a suicidal lemming.

What shocked Rafiq more was that he did the same thing himself. He had no idea where it all came from. One minute he was toying with her just for the hell of it, the next he was locked into hottest, darkest, most sexually arousing kiss he had ever experienced in his life! He could feel every quivering inch of her as if they were already naked. Her perfume filled his head, and the desperate little groans she was making as she tried to fight what was happening and knew she did not stand a chance vibrated in every one of his nerve cells.

Melanie the harlot, he thought grimly as she arched compulsively then hungrily deepened the kiss. Well...why not? he asked himself as the anger still burning within the desire gave him the excuse to do what he liked. The desk was convenient. All it would take was a lift of his arm and he could be enjoying her on a slab of cold marble. Sex in a mausoleum, he thought grimly, sacrificial and pagan. It suited him very well.

A sound beyond the door infiltrated the madness. With a tug Melanie managed to separate their mouths, then took a jerky step back. Shocked and shaken by the whole experience, she slumped weakly against the edge of the marble and gasped like a sprinter while trying to clear the dizzy fog from her head.

'What made you do that?' she choked out when she could manage to say anything.

He laughed—harshly—as if she'd just told a really bad joke. But the really bad joke was the way he was standing there calmly fastening shirt buttons she must have unfastened! Horrified, she looked down, and saw her jacket was hanging open revealing her skimpy black lace bra. Pure vanity had made her decide to wear nothing else beneath the jacket, so as not to spoil its smooth line. But now she had to deal with the mortifying knowledge that he knew she had come here only half-dressed!

As if she was begging for it. She shuddered. She could almost hear him saying those derisory words out loud. Why not? She had fallen into that kiss like a love-racked teenager.

Her skin was flushed, her nipples hard. 'I don't believe this is happening,' she breathed shakily, while urgently redoing buttons with numb fingers and wishing she couldn't still feel his hands on her body.

'You should not have come here, Melanie,' Rafiq said grimly.

'I didn't come here for this!' she cried.

'Take my advice and get out of here.' Turning, he strode back round the desk. 'And if you have any sense at all you will not attempt to come back.'

Melanie nodded in complete agreement, tried swallowing down the lump in her throat and tried to stand without the aid of the desk. It didn't happen. Her legs refused to support her. It was the final humiliation and she had to put a trembling hand up to cover her burning eyes.

He was a ruthless, heartless, arrogant devil. How could she have let herself forget all of that?

But she hadn't forgotten it. She'd merely shelved it in a box marked, Has had time to change.

'I n-need my papers,' she stammered, and in a last-ditch attempt to leave with some dignity she forced her stupid legs to carry her weight.

He nodded coolly, and began gathering the papers together. Melanie stood at his side and waited in stiff silence for him to hand them over so that she could get out of here and never, ever come back.

'Your uncle is still running the farm?' he asked suddenly.

She frowned at the question, her head still too fluffy to think properly. 'He died five years ago in a farming accident.'

'I'm sorry, I had not heard.'

Melanie shrugged away his commiserations. There had never been any affection between her and her uncle. She was sorry he had died so tragically, but other than that, she still could not bring herself to forgive him for the part he had played in trying to ruin her life.

'And Jamie?'

Ah, he couldn't resist it, could he? A fresh wave of bitterness welled, putting the light of defiance back in her eyes. Her chin went up and she threw that defiance straight at him. 'My papers,' she prompted, holding a hand out.

To Rafiq, this was a challenge and a refusal to make any comment on the person she had betrayed him with. He lowered his gaze to the outstretched hand.

'You've changed,' he remarked. 'Grown more assertive.'

'Life has a habit of changing you.'

'And money.'

'And money.' She nodded in agreement.

'Which you would like me to invest for you?'

'Money is a devil to look after if you're not used to handling it,' she answered.

'Why me?' he asked, suddenly curious when Melanie no longer wanted him to be.

'Because Randal assured me that you were the best.' And that's all you're getting out of me, she added silently.

'Liar,' he drawled. '*You* suggested *me* to Randal.'

Oh, that shook her. She hadn't expected Randal to reveal that juicy bit of information. Still, she rallied. 'Are you trying to tell me that you *aren't* the best?'

His smile this time was disturbing. Disturbing because she'd seen Robbie use the exact same expression, but had never connected it with his father before. She knew that physical things, like the colour of eyes and hair and skin, came as part of the genetic package, but she hadn't realised that smiles did also.

'There you are, then.' She tried a smile. 'I was hoping

your business ethic would put you above bearing grudges. It seems I was wrong. My mistake. I'll find someone else.'

'To…' he glanced at the top piece of paper '"…invest one half of your inheritance in long-term options while the other half is locked into a trust fund,"' he read out loud.

A frisson of alarm disturbed her breathing. He was beginning to show interest when she no longer wanted him to. 'Randal is setting the trust fund up for me,' she said tensely, her eyes fixed on those long brown fingers set against the white paper that held the details of her entire life.

Her life and Robbie's life.

'For whom?' Rafiq questioned.

'Does it matter?' she countered stiffly.

'If you want me to work with you, it does,' he murmured quietly.

'But I don't any longer.'

He ignored that and went to sit down in his chair—taking her papers with him. 'Sit and explain,' he smoothly invited, then flipped to the next page.

'N-no,' she refused. 'I've changed my mind, Rafiq. I made a mistake to come to y-you. I know that now. You were right. I should leave. I'm s-sorry I intruded.'

Rafiq narrowed his eyes on her taut stature; something inside him went very still. She was afraid, white with it, suddenly no longer defiant but teetering dangerously on the edge of panic.

'For whom?' he repeated very quietly, and watched with deepening interest as her eyes flickered away, nervously scanning anything that did not include him. They settled on the illuminated numbers on the communications console.

'Lunch is out,' she announced jerkily. 'I have to be somewhere else at one.'

Rafiq said nothing. He just continued to sit there watching as her cheeks grew even paler and her tongue made a nervous pass across trembling lips. Lips that still pulsed from his kiss, he noticed. Lips that seemed to have forgotten how to speak. She was tense, she was edgy, she was so nervous he could see the fine tremors attacking her flesh.

A sudden thought made his eyes narrow. She was Melanie Portreath now, not the Melanie Leggett he'd used to know. William Portreath had been in his nineties when he'd died, making his widow very rich. Rafiq knew how these things usually worked: wise men tended to protect their money from the machinations of a trophy wife.

But protect it for whom? 'Answer me, Melanie,' he commanded grimly.

She shimmered a glance at him then dragged it away, swallowed, and murmured huskily, 'M-my son. The trust is to be set up for my son.'

So, the old man had been capable of enjoying the charms of his lovely young bride! Rafiq's skin began to prickle at the very idea of it. She was now so pale her eyes were bruising. Was it shame? Was she beginning to realise that it was not as easy as she had expected to come in here and admit that she had sold herself for a pot of gold to a man old enough to be her grandfather?

Sickness was suddenly clawing at his stomach, disgust climbing up the walls of his chest, as she stood there staring at him through eyes that seemed to beg him for some kind of understanding. But all he saw was her beautiful, smooth naked form lying beneath a withered old man.

Placing the papers on his desk, he stood up and was amazed at the smoothness of the movement, was impressed by the way his legs carried him around the desk. 'Come with me,' he said, and was further impressed by the steadiness of his voice as he gave the instruction.

Melanie was looking slightly bewildered. He had no wish to look into her face any longer so he turned and walked away. As he strode towards the door he could hear her following him. In the outer foyer Nadia was busy at her computer, and Kadir was leaning against her desk while talking on the telephone. He was speaking Arabic, but Rafiq had not a single clue what words were being spoken in his natural tongue.

'Kadir!' With a flick of a hand he brought his aide to attention and kept on walking towards the other side of the room, where the lift stood with its doors conveniently open and waiting for them.

Kadir arrived at Rafiq's side as he was silently indicating to his aide Melanie should precede him. She was frowning as she did so, eyeing Rafiq warily as she passed him by. He ignored her to indicate to Kadir to follow suit. Kadir entered the lift. Rafiq stepped in after them, but only for as long as it took him to hit the ground-floor button. He was taking no chances here.

'Escort Mrs Portreath off the premises,' he instructed Kadir. 'And ensure that she does not gain entrance to this building again.'

With that he walked away, hearing Melanie's shocked gasp as the lift doors put solid steel between them. As he strode past Nadia's workstation he ignored his secretary's stunned expression. With the easy flow of a man completely in control of his own actions, he stepped back into his office and closed the door.

Melanie was staring at the walls of her steel prison. Shock was holding her silent and still. Beside her, the dark-haired young Arab called Kadir was almost as frozen.

She found her voice. 'What happened?' she whispered.

He offered her a very formal bow. 'I'm afraid I do not know.'

Then, before either could say anything else, the doors were opening onto the ground-floor foyer and Kadir was politely carrying out his master's wishes by escorting her all the way to the giant glass doors and even beyond. In a daze of bewilderment Melanie found herself being offered another polite bow before the young man turned and retreated through the doors again, leaving her standing there in a state of utter disabling shock at the slick smooth way

Rafiq had just executed his revenge on her—if revenge was what it had all been about. She didn't know, didn't care. He had thrown her out—publicly. In all her life she'd never felt so humiliated.

Stunned beyond being able to function sensibly, she began moving and almost fell beneath the wheels of a passing car. The car horn sounded; she just stood watching as it brushed by within inches.

Up high, in his marble tower, Rafiq viewed her near-death experience through black eyes and with bone-crackingly clenched teeth. It was only as he stood there fighting a battle between fear for her life and a wish never to lay eyes on her again that he made the connection between Melanie and the golden-haired woman he had watched hovering in the street before.

If he had known then what he knew now she would not have got beyond the building's entrance doors, saving them both a lot of trouble.

The liar, the cheat, the little slut, he seethed in ice-cold silence. And he'd had the pleasure of experiencing two of her kind in a single day! All he needed now was for his mother to rise up from the grave and tell him exactly how much money she had squeezed out of his father before she'd agreed to carry his child full term.

Money. It always came down to money with women, he concluded, as he turned away from the window after watching one of their number safely cross the road. His mobile phone began to ring. Striding over to his desk, he picked it up, opened the back, removed the SIM card, then discarded the lot into the waste-paper bin where today's Spanish newspaper was already showing yesterday's news.

By tomorrow he would have pulled the plug on Serena's finances. And his mother had ceased to be an issue when she'd died on the day of his birth. Which left only Melanie—or Mrs Portreath, he amended bitterly as he picked up the stack of her papers with the intention of consigning those to the waste-paper bin along with everything else.

Only something caught his eye and he hesitated...

CHAPTER THREE

MELANIE had no idea how she managed to get home again. She had only a vague recollection of standing on an Underground train and being strangely comforted because she was just one more blank face amongst many. But now here she stood in her own warm kitchen, surrounded by everything that represented familiarity, comfort and security to her—and she felt like an alien.

An alien being in an alien place, present, yet not a part of. It was an odd sensation, because she recognised everything yet couldn't seem to connect with any of it. The old Aga set into the chimney-breast, for instance, the scrubbed table that took up too much space but was as much a part of the family as Robbie's pictures decorating the cork notice-board on the wall by the door. Assorted mugs hung from old-fashioned cup hooks suspended beneath one of the ancient wall cabinets, and at some point since coming home, she had set the old kettle to heat on the Aga, though she didn't remember doing it. It was puffing out steam in a gentle flow now, telling her the water was hot but not yet boiling. She had lost her shoes somewhere and was standing on cold quarry tiling in silk stockings that had cost her the absolute earth, though it felt as if she was floating above the floor.

Shock. She was suffering from shock. She understood that even if she couldn't seem to do anything about it. Every time she tried to think what had thrust her into this foggy state she experienced that awful sinking sensation of a lift swooping downwards and the claustrophobic sensation of being encased in steel. But what had happened before the lift and what had come after it was refusing to show itself.

She looked at the wall clock, saw it wasn't even one o'clock yet, and realised she'd done well to get back so quickly after...

That lift swooped her downwards again and she fumbled for a kitchen chair then sank onto it, put a cold hand up to cover her mouth and caught a brief flash of Rafiq's stone-like face. She blinked slowly as the part of her brain that stored pictures refused to connect with the part that stored emotion.

He'd thrown her out.

She dropped the hand onto the table, fingertips hovering in the air as if they knew that making contact with anything solid would cause some kind of horrible calamity.

He'd played with her like a cat with a mouse. He'd insulted her, kissed her, had brought her right there to the very edge of panic by suddenly showing an interest in things she'd no longer wanted him to know about. Then, quite calmly and precisely, he had thrown her out.

Her fingers began to curl down towards the table, her stomach muscles coiled into a ball, and at last blood began to pump more oxygen to her brain. Across the kitchen the kettle began to make hissing noises; the clock on the wall chimed the hour. The fingers touched base and she stood up; it was quick and tense and impulsive.

How could she have got it so wrong? How could she have talked herself into believing that he possessed a heart worth pleading with? Where had she ever got the stupid idea that he was a worthy father for her very precious son?

The telephone mounted on the wall behind her began ringing. Forcing herself to go and answer it took most of her self-control.

'I saw you come back,' a female voice said. 'How did it go?'

It was her neighbour, Sophia. 'It didn't go anywhere,' Melanie replied, then burst into tears.

Sophia arrived within minutes, banging on the back door with a demand to be let in after having come through the hole in the hedge that separated their two gardens. She was a tall, dark-haired, sex-seething bombshell with lavender eyes and a lush mouth that could slay the world. But inside the stunning outer casing lurked a legal mind that was a sharp as a razor and as tough as the glass ceiling she was striving to break through.

'Dry those tears,' she instructed the moment Melanie opened the door to her. 'He doesn't deserve them, and you know he doesn't.'

Half an hour later Melanie had poured the whole thing out to her over a cup of tea. By then Sophia's amazing eyes had turned glassy. 'It sounds to me as if you and Robbie have just had a very lucky escape. The man is a first-class bastard. I did tell you, you should have stuck with me, kid,' she added sagely. 'I'm a much better father-figure for any boy child.'

It was such a ludicrous thing to say that Melanie laughed for the first time. But in a lot of ways Sophia was speaking the truth, because her neighbour's curt, no-nonsense approach to life had always appealed to Robbie. When he was in need of something other than his mother's loving softness he would disappear through the hole in the hedge to search out Sophia. So did Melanie, come to that.

'What did your lawyer have to say when you told him?' Sophia asked curiously. 'The same as me—I told you so?'

Randal. Melanie's brain ground to a halt again; she went still, her eyes fixed and blank. Then—

'Oh, dear God,' Melanie breathed, then jumped up and made a dive for the telephone.

'What?' Sophia demanded anxiously. 'What did I say?'

'Oh—hello.' Melanie cut across Sophia with the tense greeting. 'I need to speak to Randal Soames, please. I'm M-Mrs Portreath... W-what do you mean he isn't there? I was supposed to be meeting him there for lunch!'

'Mr Soames was called out on urgent business, Mrs

Portreath,' his secretary told her. 'I was expecting you to arrive at any minute so I could offer you his apologies.'

She didn't *want* an apology. 'I have to speak to Randal!' She was becoming hysterical. 'When will he be back?'

'He didn't say…'

'W-well…' Melanie took in a breath and tried to calm herself '…I need you to get him on his mobile phone and tell him I have s-speak to him urgently.'

'Yes, Mrs Portreath. I will try to contact him for you but I can't promise. He tends to switch off his mobile when he's in a meeting, you see.'

Melanie placed the receiver back on its rest, then sank weakly against the wall and put a hand up to cover her aching eyes.

'What was all that about?' Sophia questioned.

'I left my papers on Rafiq's desk,' she breathed. 'How could I have been so *stupid*!'

The covering hand began to tremble. On a sigh, Sophia came to place an arm across her shoulders. 'Okay, calm down,' she murmured soothingly. 'I think you need to remember that he didn't give you much chance to do otherwise,' she pointed out.

No, he hadn't, Melanie agreed. He'd just got rid of her. He'd heard enough—*had* enough—and had just got up and marched her out! Sophia almost copied him by marching her back to the kitchen table and sitting her down again, only her friend used a guiding arm to do it whereas Rafiq hadn't even spared her a glance, never mind touched her! As if she was unclean. As if he would have contaminated himself if he'd remained in her company too long.

A shudder ripped through her. 'Stop shaking,' Sophia commanded. 'The man isn't worth the grief.'

But Melanie didn't want to stop shaking. She wanted to shiver and shake and remember another time when he'd done almost the same thing. She had followed him back to London, had almost had hysterics in her desire to get inside his embassy and plead with him. What she'd met

with when she'd eventually been granted an audience had
been Rafiq locked into his Arab persona, about to attend
some formal function dressed in a dark red cloak, white
tunic and wearing a white *gut rah* on his head. He'd looked
taller and leaner, foreign and formidable. His face had
taken on a whole new appearance: harder, savage, honed
to emulate some cold-eyed, winged predator. 'Get out.'
He'd said those two immortal words then turned his back
on her to stride away.

'Melanie, if he still despises you as much as you think
he does, he will probably consign your papers to the bin
without bothering to read them.'

'Yes.' She liked that scenario.

'But would it be a very bad thing if he did read them?'
Sophia then dared to suggest. 'At least he would know
everything—which is what you wanted, remember? It was
why you decided to go to see him in the first place.'

Sophia was holding onto her hands while trying to talk
some good sense into the situation. But she hadn't been
there this morning; she hadn't seen the size of the mistake
Melanie had made. It had been huge; she'd been damned
by her own foolish optimism, letting the years soften
Rafiq's hard image until she'd actually begun to question
whether *she* had been fair to *him*.

William had helped by gently nudging her in this direction. Dear, sweet, gentle William who, like herself, hadn't
liked to see bad in anyone. But even William's advice had
only been wise with all the facts laid before him. If Rafiq
did decide to read those papers they would only tell him
half the story. As for the other half—

Well, that half belonged to his eagerness to believe
badly of her simply because people had told him to.

But, no. She sighed. There had been so much more to
it than words of poison spoken into his ear. He had *seen*
her with Jamie. It had all been so desperately damning.
And explainable, she reminded herself, if he had only
given her the chance to explain. He hadn't and still

wouldn't. That hadn't changed. He still looked at her and saw her through the unforgiving eyes of a half-Arab man with his feet firmly entrenched in cultural principles and a deep-rooted belief that all women were natural sinners.

And she no longer wanted a man like that to come anywhere near her son so he could contaminate him with his poisonous view of her.

'Melanie—'

No. She scrunched her hands free, then got to her feet. She didn't want to talk about it any more. For what was the use in talking when it was basically too late? All she could hope for now was that Randal would come through for her and manage to retrieve her stuff before Rafiq decided to feed his hatred by reading things that he really did not want to know.

'What are you doing at home at this time of the day, anyway?' she asked Sophia as an abrupt change of subject. 'I thought you were supposed to be wowing them all in some court or other.'

'The case was adjourned,' Sophia explained. 'And I'm off to wow them in Manchester tomorrow, so I decided to come home to pack a bag and catch a flight up there today. I've got friends there I haven't seen in ages—but I've changed my mind,' she then added swiftly. 'I'm going to stay here with you, just in case—'

'No, you're not.' Mouth set in a stubborn line, Melanie glared at her with a warning look. 'I had a bad experience today but I'm all right,' she insisted, and to prove it she gathered up the tea mugs and took them to the sink. 'Maybe I even needed it to help me move on from the past.'

'You believe you can do that?' Sophia sounded sceptical.

Maybe she was right to. 'I have no choice.' Just as soon as I've got my papers back, she thought with a shiver. 'Because I won't be repeating the same mistake twice.'

It was such a complete, final statement that Sophia

didn't even attempt to say another word. Ten minutes later she'd gone, leaving Melanie with the rest of the afternoon stretching out in front of her like a long dark road filled with nerve-stretching uncertainty—and a heartache she didn't want to feel.

She called Randal's office three times with no satisfaction. Actually picked up the phone to call Rafiq's secretary, only to change her mind when his final words came back to hit her full in the face. She would not even get beyond the main switchboard.

How could a man fester in such hatred that it could make him want to humiliate her like that? Tears threatened again; she swallowed them down and went upstairs to change out of her suit. As she removed the jacket she caught sight of herself in the mirror, saw the black lacy bra and relived the feeling of long brown fingers staking their claim. She shuddered, despising herself for being so easy, finished removing the suit and scrambled into a pair of faded old jeans and a roll-neck top that covered everything. By the time she walked downstairs a few minutes later she was the casual Melanie her son was used to seeing when he arrived home from school. No sign of designer clothes left anywhere for him to pick up on. No hint that she'd been doing anything today that was different from any other day.

Robbie arrived with a shout and a bump of his school bag against the polished hall floor. She turned from chopping vegetables at the sink to watch him come in through the kitchen door. His maroon and gold striped tie had flipped over his shoulder, and beneath his gaping school blazer she could see the white tails of his shirt hanging free from grey school trousers. One grey sock was up, the other was down, and his glossy black hair looked as if it had been in a fight.

Her heart dropped like a stricken bird, because even with his rumpled appearance he was hitting her hard with his father's image.

'Hi,' he said. 'Guess what we did today?'

'What?' she asked.

He frowned. 'Are you catching a cold?'

Melanie shook her head and tried swallowing the tears again. 'Just need to clear my throat.' Which she did. 'So what did you do today?' she prompted.

'We went to the park to collect fallen leaves that looked like skelintons, then took them back to press some into a books and draw round others.'

'Skeletons,' Melanie corrected.

'Skeletons,' he dutifully repeated. 'Do you want to see?'

'Of course I want to see,' she answered. 'But not before I get my hug.'

With a grin that could knock her eyes out he came towards her, a tall boy for his seven years. Melanie squatted down and opened her arms to receive him. As she hugged him close she felt another wave of emotion threaten. She must have sniffed, because Robbie jerked his head back.

Eyes as dark as his father's looked into hers, only they weren't the same, because this pair of eyes were darkened by love and warmth and concern whereas that other pair...

'Are you sure you're not catching a cold?' he demanded.

'Robbie,' she said firmly, 'I am not catching a cold, all right?'

It was a mother's voice, the I-know-everything voice. He continued to study her for a moment, then nodded his head. 'I'll go and get my bag.'

End of small developing crisis, Melanie thought with a sigh. Since William had died Robbie had lived in fear that she was going to follow him. Every sneeze, every twitch, every minor *ouch* could shake him to the core with fear.

They played with the leaves, drew some more, ate supper, watched some television then eventually went upstairs to play games in his bath before curling up on his bed to read stories. By eight o'clock he was fast asleep and Melanie had given up on expecting Randal to call.

For the next hour she tried to keep herself busy doing

the usual mundane chores. They'd used to employ a house-keeper, but she'd decided to retire when William had died and there seemed no point in employing another when there was only two of them to be looked after now. But the house was big—too big for both of them. A large Edwardian terraced home, with five bedrooms and four main reception rooms, it deserved a large noisy family to fill it, not two people who seemed to rattle around in it these days.

Melanie missed William, she missed Lucy the house-keeper, and she missed having only to open a couple of doors to find someone else there when she felt in need of company. As she felt now, she admitted, when she found herself standing in the front living room just staring into space.

Diversions, diversions, she told herself forcefully, and had just decided to go upstairs and indulge in a long hot bath in the hopes that it would ease some of the stress from her aching body when the sound of a car drawing up outside caught her ear. On legs that had suddenly turned very heavy she walked to the window and twitched back the edge of a curtain. As soon as she saw the low black monster crouching by the front gate she knew the long anxious wait was over.

Rafiq climbed out of his car and set the central locking system, then turned to view Melanie's home. It stood in the middle of an Edwardian terrace, brick-faced and solid-looking, with an iron gate leading to a small garden and a narrow porch with a half-stained-glass front door. One big bay window sat on each side of the porch and three flat windows faced the upper floor.

Did one of those windows belong to his son's bedroom?

Even thinking the word son threatened to lock him up inside. He saw a curtain twitch in a downstairs window, felt a cold winter gust of wind wipe what was left of the colour from his face.

An omen? he wondered, and had to accept that it probably was. This was not going to be easy. He was still in a deep state of shock and Randal had advised him to stay away until he had given himself time to recover. But Randal was not him. The other man could have no conception what was it was like to be him at this present moment. For how was he supposed to balance logic on the top of raging emotion? It was impossible. He was just swinging from one dark place to another with no respite in between. He had spent the whole afternoon with Randal Soames, swinging like that between a raging fury aimed entirely at Melanie and a heart-clutching sense of dismay at what he had almost tossed away today.

The curtain in a downstairs window gave a second twitch. Just before it fell back into place he caught a glimpse of Melanie's face. She had seen him. He must go in now. Had he actually been considering going away without doing so?

He didn't know, was no longer sure of anything. Half an hour ago he had been pacing his apartment; now he was here without recalling what had happened in between. He was the most controlled man he knew—prided himself on it—but control of any kind had completely deserted him. Pride, they said, usually came before a fall. Well, he was falling, had not stopped falling since he'd glanced at a piece of paper in his office and had seen the name Robert Joseph Alan Portreath typed in bold print in the middle of a blur of legal jargon.

Robert had been Melanie's father's name, but Joseph Alan belonged to him—Rafiq ben Jusef Al Alain Al-Qadim.

His throat moved on an attempt to swallow, his eyes growing glassy as he reached for the gate. It swung inwards with a creak of ageing wrought iron. As he stepped through it he caught sight of a figure through the stained-glass door and knew that Melanie was coming to open the door for him.

Don't touch the bell! Melanie prayed feverishly as she

made a last dash to get the door open before the shrill ring could fill the house and wake up Robbie.

It was like one of those nightmares where you opened the door to find yourself staring at the darkest force you could ever imagine. Big and broad and dressed entirely in black, Rafiq filled the narrow porch like a huge black shadow, blocking the light from the street behind him and taking the air from her lungs.

He believed. It was written there in every sharply angled feature, in the clench of his jaw and the muscle-locked stiffness of his big frame.

'Invite me in.'

His voice sounded like sawdust. Melanie tried to get a grip on her pounding heartbeat. 'It's late.' Like a coward she went for the easy route. 'I w-was just going to bed. W-why don't you come back tomorrow and we we'll—?'

'Invite me in, Melanie,' he repeated grimly.

'So that you can insult me again?'

'Probably.' He grimaced. 'I cannot be sure what I am going to do. I'm in shock,' he admitted.

Melanie could see it. 'All the more reason for you to come back tomorrow, when—'

His eyes gave a sudden flash. It was the only warning she got before she was being picked up by a pair of tough arms and bodily carried into the hall then into the living room.

'How dare you?' She gasped as he dropped her to her feet again.

He didn't bother to answer, instead he turned and strode back into the hallway, leaving her standing there shaking in her shoes and burning like fire down the front of her body where it had been crushed against his. She heard the front door click into its housing, heard his footsteps bringing him back this way. He stepped into the room, then closed this door also.

One look at his face here in the better light of the living room had her mentally backing away. Whatever all the hovering outside had been about, it hadn't communicated the anger she was being faced with now. He was in a rage, and a six-foot-four-inch male with a body to match his height was not what you wanted running loose in your house.

'I think y-you need to calm down a bit,' she stammered as he came towards her. 'You're in sh-shock, and you might not know w-what you're—'

'Shock,' he repeated so softly that she shivered. 'You think *this* is shock?'

'Angry, then,' she amended with a wary shrug and a gasp when the backs of her knees made contact with the arm of a chair. 'I can understand why you might feel you have the right to be. But—'

'Let us get one thing straight.' He cut across her. His mouth was thin and his eyes even narrower. 'I have the *right* to throttle the life from you for what you have done to me. But all I want from you are some acceptable answers!'

'Then back off—'

Back off? Rafiq stared down into her beautiful frightened face and blinked in complete astonishment. There was little more than an inch separating them. In fact he was standing so close she was arching her back in an effort to maintain the distance.

He was stunned. The red-hot rage had surged up out of nowhere, catching hold of him the moment he'd seen her standing at her door looking like the old Melanie, in jeans and worn-out old trainers. The years had fallen away and he'd found himself swapping new grievances for old grievances.

On a deep-throated curse he spun away from her, put a hand to the back of his neck and gripped. Behind him he could hear the uneven tug of her breathing, could feel her wariness, her fear. He closed his eyes and tried to get a hold on what was threatening to overwhelm him. He was a mess inside and the feeling was so alien that he didn't know how to deal with it.

'I apologise,' he muttered.

'It's all right,' she answered, but it was still the voice of fear.

He heard her movements as she edged warily sideways, heard the scrape of metal on metal and turned, a sense of pained horror filling him with dismay. She was standing by the fireplace and clenched in one hand was a brass poker. His eyes turned black and his stillness was suddenly electric. She believed him to be so dangerous that she armed herself against him.

'You don't need that, Melanie,' he said huskily.

He wasn't standing in her shoes, Melanie thought anxiously. He hadn't seen the look in his eyes just before he'd turned away. 'W-when you calm down I'll put it down,' she promised.

But she was shaking. Inside and out she was shaking. The way he ran those eyes over her she had a horrible feeling it would take him less than a second to disarm her if he decided to. He was big, he was strong, and he was also an expert in unarmed combat. She'd watched him in action once, in the Maitlands' all-purpose gym, when she'd gone in with a fresh stack of towels, only to find herself pulled to a complete standstill by the sight of him stripped to the waist and sparring with his brother. Sheikh Hassan had been stripped to the waist too, but she couldn't recall what he looked like. Only this man, moving with a speed and dexterous grace that belied his size and weight. He'd seen her standing there and had stopped to stare; within seconds he'd been flat on his back with his brother pinning him there. 'Such distraction is very unfair,' he'd sighed out complainingly and, as Sheikh Hassan had glanced up to see what he was talking about their positions had been smoothly reversed.

Man pitched against man, power against power, slick and smooth and so inherently masculine, with rippling muscles and the gleam of their bronzed flesh and the scent of the efforts permeating the air. She'd turned and run.

As Rafiq began walking towards her now maybe she should do the same thing, she told herself. But she couldn't run this time. This was her home. Her son lay sleeping upstairs. So she tightened her grip on the poker until her knuckles showed white, then made ready to defend herself.

His eyes were dark, his eyelashes lying thick against his cheekbones, his mouth a grim straight line. She sucked in a gulp of air as he reached out and closed a hand round the poker. With a gentle twist it was taken from her fingers.

'Never brandish point-on,' he said gravelly. 'The first thrust will tear your arm from its socket. Use it like this.' While she stood too dazed to stop him, he took hold of her hand, placed the poker back into it, angled it across her breasts, then, with a speed that set her gasping, he jerked the poker in a slashing arc towards his body. It came to stop with the point a breath away from his neck. 'This way you have a chance of doing me some damage.'

It was mad, really stupid, but her mouth began to wobble and tears suddenly filmed her eyes. 'I don't want to damage you,' she breathed shakily.

'I know.' He released his grip on the poker. 'It was my fault. I frightened you.' With that he turned and walked towards the door.

'Wh-where are you going?'

'You were right. I should not have come here tonight,' he answered grimly. 'I will go and leave you with your... safety.'

'N-no!' she cried, and wondered why. She wished she could stop trembling and tried to calm herself. 'Y-you're here now and...'

He stopped halfway across the room. Silence arrived. It pulled and it prodded. Melanie gripped the poker and tried to think of something to say that would not cause another eruption.

'Would you like a drink?' was her only inspiration. 'I can soon…'

'No—thank you,' he refused.

'Your jacket, then—let me take your jacket.' It was made of the softest kind of leather, his trousers of the smoothest suede. She swallowed thickly.

As she made to walk forward she was stopped when he turned to show her what was written in his eyes. 'I would really like to see my son.'

His son. The huskily possessive sound of his words had a creasing effect on her stomach. 'He's asleep. I don't want—'

'I was not intending to wake him, just…look upon him. Is that too much to ask?'

There was a bite to the last part. Without it she might well have given in, but the bite told her that his mood was still unpredictable. So she shook her head. 'He's a very light sleeper. The last thing he needs it to wake up and find a stranger standing over him.'

'Whose fault is it that I am a stranger?'

She ignored that. 'You need to understand a few things before we bring Robbie into this.'

'Such as the fact that you were never married to William Portreath?'

'I never said that I was,' she denied.

'You allowed me to assume it.'

'I don't recall being given the time to let you build any assumptions,' she countered coolly.

He took the criticism with a straightening of his shoulders. Melanie turned to put the poker back on its stand, but changed her mind and began stabbing at the fire log instead. Given a choice, he would rather be anywhere else than here in this room having this conversation with her, she reminded herself as wood sparks began to fly. In his eyes she was nothing, just a piece of low life he believed he had rid himself of once and for all today. Now he was being forced to backtrack, to be contrite and polite and civilised when he felt like being neither.

She made another hard stab at the fire log.

More sparks flew around the grate. 'You changed your name from Leggett to Portreath.'

'It pleased William to know that Robbie would carry on the Portreath name,' she explained.

The air was suddenly as tight at a bowstring, and Melanie knew why. He was thinking about Robbie's right to carry on *his* name. But, by the grim way he pressed his lips together, she realised he was not going to make any comment—for now at least.

Instead he stuck to his original subject. 'You call yourself *Mrs* Portreath,' he stated. 'Does this not signify a married status?'

'Why are *you* so struck by my marital status?' she countered, putting the poker back on its rest then turning to frown at him. 'I'm an unmarried mother with a son's feelings to consider,' she reminded him defensively. 'It made life simpler for Robbie if I invented a dead husband.'

'And a dead father.'

'I didn't say that,' Melanie denied. 'He knows about you. Of course he does. It would be unforgivable of me to pretend you were dead just because—'

'He knows who I am?' For such a dark-skinned man he suddenly looked ashen.

'Yes,' she confirmed. 'It was only natural that he should ask and only right that I should tell him the truth. But he—'

Rafiq's response shook her—she just didn't see it coming—so when he dropped down into one of the sofas then buried his face in his hands she was shocked.

'Rafiq...'

'No.' He shook his head. 'Leave me a moment.'

But he needed more than a moment to come to terms with what was suddenly raging inside him. His son knew about him. He knew he had a father who had never bothered to come and see him.

He couldn't make up his mind if it would have been less painful to think the boy had believed him dead!

'You have to understand. Robbie only—'

'Shut up,' he rasped, and found anger again, found strength in it, then lifted his dark head. 'I want to break your deceitful neck for keeping my son from me!' he ground out.

'You had your chance to be a father, Rafiq, and you blew it, not me.'

'When?' He was suddenly on his feet again. '*When* did you give me this chance?'

'When you threw me out of your embassy eight years ago!'

'You knew then and said nothing?'

Melanie laughed. 'You were the man who told me it was no use my saying a single word because you wouldn't believe me anyway!'

'And you could not bring yourself to stand your ground and *insist* I listen to you?'

Chin up, eyes bright, face white and body trembling, she still held her ground. 'For what purpose?' she demanded. 'You would have still called me a liar.'

A flick of a hand brought contempt back into the fight. 'You were sleeping with your step-cousin. Of course I would have questioned the boy's parentage!'

If Melanie had still had the poker in her hand she would have hit him with it. Who did he think he was, standing here trying to lay all the blame on her? 'What if I *had* come to you with your son in my arms, Rafiq?' she challenged. 'What if I'd said, Look, Rafiq, see for yourself that this child belongs to you?' She released a bitter little laugh. 'I'll tell you what you would have done. You would have taken him away from me. You would have used your filthy billions to split me from my child!'

'I would not!' He actually dared to look shocked.

Melanie wasn't impressed. 'Yes, you would,' she insisted. 'You believed I was a cheap little slut and a gold-digger who had made an utter fool out of you. You would have wanted revenge—probably still want it!' she flashed. 'But I have my own money with which to fight you now. I also have Robbie, who *loves* me, Rafiq. He loves *me*, as his mother, and he's old enough and wise enough to hate anyone who might dare to try and pull us apart!'

He went paler with every bitter word she tossed at him, until a white ring circled his taut mouth. 'If you feel like this, why have you decided to bring me into his life?'

'Because he needs you,' she whispered.

'And did not need me before?'

'No.' She shook her head. 'Before, he had William.'

CHAPTER FOUR

RAFIQ turned away as if her answer had cut him. His action more or less said it all for Melanie. Her anger fled, leaving her feeling weak and shaken, and she too turned away, putting a hand up to cover her trembling mouth, and waited for him recover from what she'd thrown at him. Because she knew it wasn't over, not by a long way.

Neither moved nor tried to speak again. In the drumming silence Rafiq was trying to decide how he felt about these latest revelations, and realised he was in no fit state to attempt the problem. Or was he being a coward and delaying the ugliness of truth?

And what was that truth? he asked himself. The truth was that Melanie had accused him of things he couldn't argue with. He would not have believed her son was his, unless presented with positive evidence. He would certainly have moved heaven and earth to remove his son from the clutches of a woman he believed unfit to rear his child.

He still believed it, which only helped to make the situation that bit uglier.

'I think I should leave,' he heard himself murmur.

'Yes,' she agreed.

'I think we should defer the rest until another time when we are both...calmer.'

'Yes,' she agreed again.

Yet he didn't move—he wanted to move but something was stopping him. A need to stay? To be here where his son was? Or was it Melanie who was holding him? He turned to look at her, at the fall of her pale hair against slender shoulders that were no longer straight with defiance but hunched and heavy. Her black woollen top clung to the gentle curves of her body and the jeans followed the lines of her hips and thighs. She held a hand to her mouth, he saw, which explained why her answers had sounded muffled, and the other hand was wrapped around her body, the fingernails trembling where they dug deep into black wool.

He turned away again, and looked at the room for the first time since he'd entered it. It came as a small surprise. The décor was old-fashioned, the furniture the same, mostly heavy dark pieces that spoke of another era, like the patterned red carpet that covered the floor and the dark red velvet curtain fabric that matched the upholstery covering the sofas and chairs. It was a man's kind of room, warm and solid, with the odd female touch, such as the jewel-coloured silk cushions heaped on the sofas and chairs.

He liked it, which further surprised him because he was so predisposed to dislike anything to do with Melanie right now.

Or was it William Portreath's taste he was reluctantly admiring? he then wondered suddenly, and felt the bitterness well up again, felt the hard cut of envy for a man who had loved another man's child enough to present him with his own name.

He didn't want to leave. Melanie could feel his reluctance wrapping round the room like a heavy dark cloud that stole all the oxygen. He was still steeped in shock. His son was here in this very house. He needed to see him, see the truth for himself. She understood that, and wished so much that things had worked out differently this morning, because they could have got all the fighting out of the way then and he could have happily met Robbie and have seen what a wonderful child they had made together. More importantly, Robbie would have met his father and would have known that he was no longer in danger of being left alone in this world if anything should happen to her.

Should she say something—hold out yet another olive branch? Should she tell him that she understood how he was feeling, but that she had to protect both herself and her son?

Would he listen? Was he ready to do that now?

A log dropped in the grate and sent out a spray of crackling sparks. As it did so the Westminster mantel clock chimed the hour. Then a floorboard creaked somewhere, making Melanie turn to look at the door. Sensing her doing it, Rafiq did the same thing. It came again; the pair of them went so still they could hear their hearts beating. Melanie knew every bump and creak in this old house; she knew every draught and whistle.

'What?' Rafiq asked.

'Robbie,' she said, and started walking. 'Stay in here,' she cautioned as she opened the door. Then she disappeared, closing the door behind her without seeing that Rafiq was incapable of going anywhere.

He had frozen into a posture only his brother would recognise. But even Hassan had only seen it happen when it involved their father and his battles with death that were sometimes too close to call. The name of it was fear—fear of losing a man he loved above all else in this world—only here he was experiencing the same paralysed fear of meeting his seven-year-old son.

Would she do that? Would Melanie bring the boy down here and present them to each other without any preparation to ease the—?

Another log fell in the grate and broke him free from his stone-like stasis. He turned his head and saw the log was in danger of rolling into the hearth.

Robbie was just coming out of the bathroom when Melanie arrived on the upstairs landing. 'Okay?' she asked softly.

'Mmm,' he murmured sleepily. 'I thought I heard voices.'

'The television, probably.' Melanie smiled through the

untruth and walked with him into his bedroom, then helped to tuck him into bed.

'I had a dream tonight, but it wasn't a bad one,' he told her.

'Good.' She stroked his silk dark head.

'There was a man on a big black stallion and he stopped and said, ''Are you Robbie?'' I said, ''Yes'' and he smiled and said, ''Next time, you can ride up here with me, if you like.'''

'Well, that was nice of him.' Melanie smiled, thinking she didn't like the idea of some stranger offering her son rides.

'Mmm.' His eyes were drooping; he gave a yawn. 'He was wearing one of those white robes and had a thing on his head, like Arabs wear.'

Melanie's stomach rolled over. She wasn't one of those people who believed dreams forecast the future, and Robbie knew about his Arabian side because William had spent hours with him in his study, filling his mind with all things Arabian. No doubt there had been a picture of an Arab on horseback at some time. But for her son to have the dream tonight of all nights disturbed her more than she liked.

'Go back to sleep,' she whispered.

'You won't go anywhere, will you?'

'No, I won't go anywhere,' she softly promised. 'Except back downstairs to watch television,' she added, just in case he was expecting her to remain right here, kneeling beside his bed for the rest of the night. It had happened before and probably would again, she mused bleakly.

But not tonight, she saw as he dropped back into sleep without another murmur. She waited a few minutes longer to make sure he was fully asleep, though, taking no chances in a situation that was hazardous enough as it stood without Robbie deciding to follow her downstairs as she knew he was quite capable of doing. But eventually she rose up and left him, silently closing the bedroom door behind her—just in case voices became raised again.

Walking back into the living room required her to take a deep breath for steadiness. What she found was that Rafiq had removed his jacket to reveal a black cashmere roll-neck sweater and was squatting down in front of the fire. His body twisted when he heard her come in, eyes fiercely guarded as they shifted across the empty spaces at her sides. Tension screamed from every muscle, from every flicker of an eyelash. He was looking for Robbie.

'He got up to use the bathroom,' she explained quickly. 'Then fell asleep again almost as soon as he'd climbed back into bed.'

With a nod of his head Rafiq turned away again, but not before she'd seen a war between desire and relief taking place upon his face, and her heart gave a twist of sympathy for this man who had to be struggling with just about every emotion available to him.

It was only as she began to walk forward that she noticed he held the hearth brush and pan in his hands. She also noticed the stretch of fine wool across expanded shoulder blades and remembered what it had felt like to press against them with the flat of her palms. Heat began to pool low down in her stomach; memories that really should not be so clear and sharp after all of these years sent her eyes on a journey down the length of his spine to the leanness of his hips and the power in his spread thighs.

'A log fell onto the hearth,' he said as she came up beside him. His voice sounded rough, like gravel. He wasn't actually using the brush and pan because he was just squatting there, staring at them as if they weren't there.

Coming down beside him, Melanie took them from his loose fingers and laid them aside. 'Rafiq...I'm sorry for saying what I said before. I was angry, and—'

'You needed to say those things, and I suppose I needed to hear them.'

But he wasn't sure. She watched the firelight play with

his taut features and enrich the dark olive tones of his skin. 'Here,' she said, and dipped a hand into the pocket in her jeans, then gently slotted a photograph into one of his hands. 'I thought you might like to have this.'

It was Robbie, looking all grown-up and smart in his school uniform and wearing that familiar rather sardonic half-smile. It had occurred to her as she was coming back down the stairs that Rafiq still had no conception of how like him his son was. If she had taken him into William's study he would have seen Robbie's face laughing back at him from photos on every available surface, because that was the way William had liked it and she hadn't yet got around to moving anything—hadn't had the heart to change anything anywhere in the house.

'It was taken in school only a few weeks ago,' she explained. 'He looks so much like you that it came as a shock when I walked into your office this morning and realised just...'

Her voiced trailed away, dying on words that did not need saying because she could tell from Rafiq's reaction that he was seeing it all for himself. His eyes were fixed on the simple four-by-four portrait. She could hear the strain in his shallow breathing, feel the tension in his body and the pulsing, stinging agony of his stress.

She tried to swallow, but found it impossible. She felt the sudden need to give him some space and privacy for what was battering him, but couldn't bring herself to get up and move away. Tears thickened her throat; her chest began to feel too tight. In desperation she reached out to pick up the hearth brush and pan and began carefully gathering up fine flakes of wood ash still scattered on the grate.

It was dreadful. Say something, she wanted to beg him. Shout at me, if you like! But I need to know what you think of this beautiful child we made together. I need—

His hands came out and took back the brush and pan. As her breathy gasp filtered through the air she watched him lay them carefully aside. She didn't know what was coming—was afraid of what was coming. Especially when long lean fingers curled around her upper arms and began drawing her to her feet. She felt small suddenly, overwhelmed by his superior height and size. He was standing too close, his touch achingly gentle yet frighteningly disturbing. The heat of his breath was on her face and his thighs were touching hers. Her arms felt soft and frail beneath the controlled power in his imprisoning fingers, and her breasts were tingling at the nearness of his chest.

Wary, she lifted her eyes to his, and the breath shivered from her lips at what she saw written in the dark glitter of his eyes.

No, she wanted to protest, but the denial just wouldn't come, and it would have been too late anyway because his dark head lowered and he was kissing her, though not hard or hotly as he had this morning. Nor even because he felt driven by a simple need to make physical contact with another human being right now. He was kissing her with reverence, gently crushing her against him, gently crushing her mouth with his.

Then he released her and turned away, dark head slightly lowered, wide shoulders set. He picked up his jacket, then just walked out of the room and, seconds later, out of the house, leaving Melanie standing right where he had left her, with the warmth of his kiss still pulsing against her lips and what she'd seen in his eyes before he turned away, quietly tearing her apart.

Tears, she'd seen the hot black glint of tears in the eyes of a man who'd gone way beyond the point of being able to contain the power of what it was he had been forced to deal with today.

She had done that. With her little plots and shock strategies she had managed to reduce a proud man to tears in front of her. She had never felt so ashamed of herself.

Rafiq sat in his office staring down at the neatly processed, finely detailed document he had spent the whole night working on. He was good at this, he acknowledged with absolutely no sense of pleasure. Concentrating his talents on the detached and inanimate was most definitely his forte. Money instead of emotions. The planning and arranging of someone else's finances instead of allowing himself to lie in his bed crucifying himself with his inadequacies as a fully paid up member of the human race.

The phone on his desk began to ring, halting the urge to put his head back and close his sleep-starved eyes. It was Randal Soames. 'Are you sure you want this?' the lawyer asked him.

'Exactly as I have set it out,' he confirmed.

He sounded dubious. 'You might marry some day, have more children.'

Not this man, Rafiq thought bleakly. 'Have you spoken to Melanie?'

Swift change of subject. He could almost hear Randal thinking it. 'She isn't there. There is some kind of function on at the boy's school, I seem to recall. I'll try again later.'

The boy's school. Some kind of function. Just two more things about his son he had no knowledge of.

Oh, damn. He got up and swung away from his chair, shoved his hands into his trouser pockets, then stood staring out of the window at a cold grey day. It had now begun to pour with rain.

Safely slotted into his wallet rested a miniature image of himself at the age of seven. Similar hair, similar eyes, similar slightly rueful expression which hid the same vulnerability he had suffered at the same age. He felt as if he knew this child of his inside out, yet he could not say which school his dark red uniform represented, nor what the boy ate for breakfast each morning.

His son even had his skin shading. So where were Melanie's genes? Where was his French blood? Where was there anything in the photograph to say that his son had not been cloned on a scientist's bench instead of conceived during the act of love?

Love. He cursed the word, hated it—despised it—and felt it grinding against his every muscle like a physical torture set up to make him accept that love could beat the hell out of any man's wish to feeling nothing.

He was in love with his son, but had made no attempt to go anywhere near him. He loved his father, his brother, and Hassan's lovely wife, Leona—but differently. With them he felt safe to love; with the boy he did not. Which was why he was standing here preferring to stare at the rain than take the bull by the horns and face uncertainty.

As for Melanie…

A sigh shot from him at this other reason why he had spent the past two days simmering in his own confusion. He had loved Melanie when they had conceived their son, but he would prefer not to be reminded of it. Now, what came next? Where were they supposed to go? Into one of those awful situations he had witnessed amongst so many friends with broken relationships, where they shared the children by cool agreement—when there was nothing damn cool about a child's feelings?

A knock sounded on his door; he swung round to watch Kadir walk in the room. As his aide offered a bow of apology for intruding Rafiq caught the sparkle of raindrops on the shoulders of his neat grey jacket. 'Been out in this filthy weather, Kadir?' he quizzed.

'Yes, sir.' Rafiq received another bow. 'A note has just arrived for you,' Kadir explained, and walked forward to hold it out to him.

Rafiq looked down at it without attempting to take it, wearily wondering, What now? Because this was no formal business note. The envelope was small and square, and its sender female, by the neatly scripted way his name had been written upon it. No address or postage stamp, which said it had been hand-delivered.

'Who is it from?'

Kadir cleared his throat. 'It arrived in another envelope addressed to me. This is all I know.'

All he knew. Frowning, Rafiq pulled his hands out of his pockets and accepted the letter, then he broke the glued seal. Still frowning, he took out the single sheet of paper and read the two short sentences written upon it. 'Can I come up? I'm standing across the street.'

His heart hit against his ribcage. He swung back to the window to stare down through sheets of rain to the street. A solitary figure stood against the building opposite, sheltering from the rain beneath a big black umbrella.

Melanie. Something burst into life inside him. With a twist of his body he snatched his jacket off the back of his chair. 'Have my car waiting,' he instructed Kadir as he headed for the door—then paused as his mind made a connection. 'Don't make a habit of lying to me, Kadir,' he advised.

Then he left, with Kadir's rather heavy, 'No, sir,' hanging in the air.

The lift took him downwards; his feet took him outside. The sheeting rain drenched him in the few seconds it took him to cross the street.

Melanie only realised he was there when she saw his feet appear in front of her. The umbrella was wrenched from her fingers, and was held higher, so he could join her beneath it. She looked up and saw the strain in his face, the tiredness, the frown. 'Are you mad?' he demanded. 'Why are you standing out here?'

'I didn't want your security people throwing me off the premises,' she explained. 'But I needed to talk to you.'

By the way he flattened his mouth she assumed he'd forgotten about his instructions regarding her and his bank. Then he noticed that she was shivering so much her teeth were chattering and, taking a grim hold on her arm, he hustled her into the nearest doorway, snapped the umbrella shut and laid it aside. Then he removed his jacket and swung it around her shoulders.

'You're freezing,' he muttered. 'I cannot believe you came here dressed like this.'

She was in her designer suit again. It had seemed appropriate when she'd made the decision to come. Now she was so grateful for the added warmth of his jacket that she huddled greedily into it. 'It w-wasn't raining this much when I left home and—and I'm not thinking very clearly right now…'

'I understand the feeling,' he murmured dryly.

'Now y-you're wet too,' she continued in an agitated rush. 'Y-you should have got Kadir to—'

'Run a few more messages?' he offered when she tried to swallow her runaway tongue.

She glanced up, met his eyes, saw the sardonic gleam in them and released a sigh. 'He told you. He promised he wouldn't. I didn't want him to get into trouble for colluding with me.'

'You believed I would be angry with him?'

'It's been two days…' Two days of waiting and pacing and jumping out of her skin every time the doorbell or telephone rang. In the end she hadn't been able to take the stress any longer and had come to find him. Now she wished that she hadn't because she was feeling like a fool.

'Kadir carried out your instructions to the letter,' Rafiq inserted. 'As for the rest…I guessed.'

He'd guessed. 'Mr Omnipotent,' she muttered.

To her surprise he laughed, it was a low deep sound that brought her eyes fluttering up to his again, which were warm and dark and concentrated on her. Things began to happen she just didn't want, like a pooling of warmth deep down in her abdomen and a breathlessness that tightened her chest.

Don't look at me like that, she wanted to protest, but too many things were leaping between them, such as the son they shared, not to mention shared kisses. Intimacy, in other words; too much of it that went back too many years yet could tug on her senses as if everything, including the events leading to Robbie's conception, had happened only yesterday.

'I needed time to think,' he murmured huskily.

Husky suddenly made her clothes feel too tight. 'I know you m-must be hurt, but I h-had to protect myself.'

'From the omnipotent Arab with revenge on his mind?' He smiled as he said it, but it was a grim smile.

'I'm sorry, but, yes,' she answered honestly. 'You—'

His hand lifted up to push a stray coil of damp hair away from her temple and she responded with a tense little jerk. Beyond the shelter of the doorway, the rain pounded on the pavements. The coil of hair left a trailing raindrop behind it so his finger moved to scoop it from her cheek.

Someone dashed into the doorway, stopped to shake out their umbrella, then, with a curious glance at them both, walked into the building, leaving Melanie with the disturbing impression that she must look like a wicked woman snatching a secret assignation with her tall dark lover.

Lowering her eyes, she huddled further into his jacket. It was big on her—huge—the slippery silk lining whispering softly against the thin fabric of her suit. She was picking up the scent of his aftershave from it, subtle and spicy, tantalisingly familiar. He couldn't stand much closer to her if he tried.

Maybe Rafiq was thinking along similar lines, because he released a short sigh. Her eyes became fascinated with his slender red tie and the way it lay down the length of his white shirt, covering muscular proportions that expanded and contracted with the sigh.

Her lips began to pulse, and it scared the life out of her. Things were happening here that really should not. 'I don't think this is an appropriate place,' she said a little wildly.

'No,' he agreed, but made no move to do anything about it.

One of those silences fell; it pumped up her heartbeat and dried out her mouth. His hands began to move, sliding beneath the lapel of his navy blue jacket until the backs of his fingers came to rest against her breasts. She pulled in a sharp breath; for a fine tight nerve-singing moment she thought he was going to lower his head and kiss her.

Then she shivered as genuine cold made itself felt again, and he was setting her free to reach for the umbrella. Opening it up, he urged her beneath it, then out into the pouring rain. Her stiletto shoes danced puddles as he hurried her across the street. Expecting to be ushered into the bank, she was surprised to find herself being bundled into the back of a car. It was big and plush, with a glass partition between them and the driver, and seats made of soft black leather.

Through shivering chatters she watched Rafiq toss the umbrella onto the floor of the car, then climb in beside her. His shirt was wet, showing patches of dark skin beneath its white fabric and his black hair was soaked and slicked to his head. He leant forward to pick up a telephone, uttered some terse command in Arabic, then sat back with a sigh.

'Where are we going?' she questioned.

'Somewhere we can talk.'

'Oh.' She took a pensive glance out of the window. 'I thought the bank…'

'No,' he said, and that was all. Her top teeth pressed into her bottom lip because she wasn't sure she liked the sound of that no.

'Rafiq—'

'Randal has been trying to contact you.'

A diversion. 'Has he?'

'He said you were out at some function or other.'

'First thing this morning, yes.' She nodded. 'Robbie's school is putting on a pantomime at Christmas. They're doing *Cinderella*. There were rehearsals this morning. I—helped out.'

'Which school?'

She told him. He pressed his lips together and nodded his dark head. Melanie shifted tensely, unsure of his mood now and even more uncertain that she wanted to be sitting here in such close confines with a man she couldn't read from one second to the next.

For all she knew he could be sitting here plotting her downfall—or her seduction. Because something improper had been running through his mind back there in the doorway. It had been running through hers too, she was forced to admit. It just wasn't fair. Only this man had ever been able to toss her into this hectic state of sexual awareness just by—being there.

She frowned at the rain-spattered window. That feeling had been there from the first time her arm had brushed against his shoulder when she'd been serving him at the Maitlands' dinner table. Twenty years old, as naive as they came, she'd caught his scent, the sound of his low dark laughter and the deeply smooth voice tones as he'd spoken to the person sitting next to him, and her response had been so primitively sexual that she'd spilled the sauce onto the tablecloth.

After that had come the humiliating dressing down from Sally Maitland, then her first real contact with his hand, when Rafiq had cornered her later and tried to make light of the embarrassing incident. He'd been dressed in a dinner suit, big and dark, suave and sophisticated, with an easy grace that had belied his size and a lazily worn self-confidence that aimed to charm.

'Watch him,' Sally Maitland had warned later. 'Arab men are notoriously attracted to slender young blondes. He'll take what you are putting on offer, Melanie, then despise you for it later.'

She had been right, too. Rafiq had pursued her like a man besotted until he'd finally managed to break down her defences. He'd promised her everything: love, marriage, the whole wonderful package. But the moment he'd taken what he had really been after he'd despised her for giving it. He'd seen a tramp then, a woman willing to give it out to all and sundry once she'd acquired the taste.

He moved. She stiffened and swung her head round to send him a hard, accusing glance.

'What?' He looked shocked by it.

'Nothing.' She looked away again, hoping to goodness that eight years of abstinence had given her some defence against him, though why did she think she needed it?

Because Rafiq still desired her. It had been there when they'd met in his office two days ago, there when he'd come to her home. It had been there just now in the doorway when he'd almost given in to it and kissed her.

Three meetings, two kisses, and one still hovering on the sidelines with time on its side to give it a chance.

As for defences, they were not much use when she only had to look at him to feel that old breathless, sensual pull.

The car drew to a stop outside a block of select apartments. Life took another worrying twist when she realised where they had to be. Rafiq opened his door and braved the rain again to stride round to her side of the car and open her door.

'I don't think...'

His hand found her wrist and the jacket began to slip from her shoulders as he tugged her into the rain. As she grappled to save the jacket from falling onto the wet pavement he pulled her inside the building before she had a chance to voice a bigger protest.

A man dressed in a security uniform sat behind a desk. He stood up and smiled. 'Good morning, sir...madam,' he greeted politely. 'Dreadful weather,' he opined with a glance at their rain-soaked clothes.

Rafiq murmured a reply; Melanie offered a nervous little smile and wondered what the man must really be thinking as Rafiq pulled her into the lift.

'I don't think this is a good idea,' she protested a trifle breathlessly.

'I do,' he countered, and one glance at him told her why he did. He wasn't even trying to hide it!

A wave of answering heat put her into a panic. 'No,'

she said, and tried to twist her wrist free from his grasp so she could turn and make a diving exit before the lift doors closed. But Rafiq was one step ahead of her; with only the gentlest of tugs he brought her hard up against his body at the same time as his other hand snaked out to hit the lift button.

To the man on the desk they must have looked like two people so hungry for each other they couldn't wait until they were alone. The lift doors closed while Melanie was still trying to recover from the shock contact with Rafiq's body. Eyes like hot coals burned his intention; her blood began to race, charged by her hammering heartbeat.

'How dare you?' she choked in shrill protest. 'This is supposed to be about Robbie!'

Rafiq laughed. Maybe she was right, but he didn't think so. For two long days he had prowled through his life trying to understand what it was that was holding him back from going to meet his son. For two aching days and sleepless nights he'd swung from one reason to another without hitting upon the right one. But one look at Melanie standing in the rain and the answer had lit up in his head like a beacon. He could not deal with the problem of his son until he'd dealt with the problem of his son's mother. He wanted her—all of her. He wanted every single thing he had walked away from eight years ago. He wanted her in his life, in his bed! And the best thing about it was that he meant to have it all, without the love thing cluttering up his reasoning.

'I am going to take you in my arms and kiss you stupid,' he informed her grittily. 'I am going to strip the clothes from your body and enjoy your exquisite flesh. I will take you to my bed and avail myself of every sweet, delectable inch of you,' he rasped with husky incision. 'I am going to take you out and buy you a ring which will say that you belong to me. Then, and only then, I will take you with me to meet my son! You owe me this much, Melanie-of-the-sweet-face-and-lying-little-heart. You owe me for eight long years of bitterness, and seven years of never knowing my son!'

CHAPTER FIVE

'YOU'RE crazy,' she breathed as she strained to get away from him.

'Maybe.' He shrugged, but the look in her eyes told him she was captivated by the whole exciting agenda, and she was quivering against him like a trapped little bird, mesmerised and enthralled.

'How long has it been for you, Melanie, since a man laid his hands on your body?' he questioned darkly. 'How long since you felt the burning thrust of a man's pleasure zone driving you mindless with need?'

Her mouth was trembling, her eyes were bright, her skin pale with what might have been mistaken for fear if it hadn't been for the seductive scent of her arousal sweetening the air. He knew that scent, had picked up on it at their first meeting, and it had never failed to be there every time they'd been near each other since. Eight years had not changed it; eight years had not diminished one small part of what it could do to him.

'Sex...' He leant close to whisper. 'It is all around us. You can feel it. Stop pretending.'

'If you don't stop this I am going to start screaming!'

His response was to clasp his free hand round her nape, his eyes glittering his intention just before he lowered his dark head and took what he wanted: her mouth, her hot, dry, trembling mouth, that opened without pause to welcome him. Her fingers grappled with his shirt front; her breasts heaved against his chest. And as her beautiful thighs arched in their eagerness to make contact with his, it was Melanie who plunged into the kiss.

She groaned as his tongue caressed moist tissue. He

laughed, low and throatily deep, pulsing with dark triumph that brought her nails clawing into his neck in punishment. He didn't care. He liked those sharp nails digging into him. They let him know this could be as wild and unbridled as he wanted it to be. They made him feel alive, energised! With Serena it had been sex. With this woman it was—regeneration of every single cell he possessed!

The lift doors slid apart. Without breaking the kiss, he swung her up into his arms and carried her towards his apartment door. Opening it with the key was a struggle when he was not prepared to release her mouth, but he managed it, stepped inside, kicked the door shut behind him then, with a satisfied grunt, began walking down the hallway towards the only room that mattered right now.

His jacket slipped from her shoulders, trailed its way to the ground and was left where it fell as he walked with unerring steps into the bedroom and shut this door too. Which left only them and a giant-sized bed, standing proud with its cover of royal blue silk. No soft feathers this time, no deep eiderdown, just a firm flat mattress dressed in the perfect colour on which to lay his prize.

When he lowered her feet to the floor she was trembling so badly she could barely stand upright unaided. Her eyes were big, glazed, and the colour of the richest gold, her mouth full and red and begging for his.

'Now tell me no.' He laid the silken words down like a challenge.

She couldn't answer. When all she did was reach out a hand to steady herself, he caught it and placed it onto his chest. Her eyes flickered down to absorb the fact that she was touching hair-roughened flesh. She had done it again. Without knowing it she'd unfastened his shirt during their walk down the hall!

'Yes,' he breathed in dark confirmation, and yanked his tie loose then tossed it aside. The last shirt button came undone at his throat and the shirt fell wide open to reveal a body built to carry the world if it was ever called upon to do so.

'Oh, dear God,' she managed to breathe in shaken realisation. By then his fingers were unfastening the buttons of her jacket to reveal a fitted top she had added to the ensemble that had not been there the last time.

Protection from him, or herself? The jacket slid from her shoulders; the top slipped over her head. As she lifted those dazed eyes back up to his he kissed her, fiercely, just in case she decided to try and stop this.

But Melanie was in no fit state to stop anything. She was lost in a gripping love affair with this man's body and the power of his kiss. Every time she breathed she drowned in the scent of him; every time she moved she felt the impact of his strength. His mouth consumed her with a voracious hunger; the stroke of his hands collapsed her brain. She had no sense, no will, no desire to do anything but be here, feeling the raging torment of a need so potent it overwhelmed her. The eight years since she'd been with him like this didn't seem to matter. Her senses remembered, desired and demanded she feed them with everything.

'This is mad,' she whimpered.

He didn't answer. His hands were ridding her of her bra. The black lace drifted away from full rounded breasts with nipples already tightly distended. He touched; she groaned and simply fell against him, then fell again, into a pit packed full of sensation. Sleek bronzed skin electrified her fingers; the rasp of curling hair excited her breasts. The kiss was a seduction on its own hot merits, and as he slid down the zip of her skirt she wriggled her hips to aid its journey to the floor. The powerhouse thrust of his erection jumped as she writhed against him. His breathing was rough, his body clenched by the ferocity of his desire. But when he slid his hands beneath the final piece of black lace to tug her more firmly against him, she was the one to fall apart.

It was a complete loss of control. She cupped his face, kissed it all over, urgently, desperately touching and tasting, and forcing tight, thick sounds to rasp from his throat. He belonged to her. This man, this glorious dark-skinned giant, belonged to her. She'd believed it eight years ago and she believed it again now. Part of her might be yelling, *Fool!* but at this precise moment she didn't care.

His hands spanned her hips and lifted her up against him; her arms wound around his neck. He began carrying her again, to lower her down onto the firm cool expanse of the large bed. Warm skin slid against the smoothness of silk; long limbs stretched sensually. Her eyes caught a glimpsing impression of ivory presented on a bed of blue, with her hair a golden halo as she watched him divest himself of the rest of his clothes. She watched in fascination as he drew in tight muscles in his abdomen then unclipped his trousers; her mouth ran dry as she watched him slide down the zip. Two seconds later he was naked, and her insides were curling on a mixture of excitement and stark, staring alarm until she remembered how it felt to absorb this man into her.

Then he was lowering his big frame down right next to her, reaching out to roll her against him. Skin met skin, stealing her breath away. His mouth claimed hers and his hands began to wreak magic, shaping her breasts, her stomach, the sensitive inner flesh of her thighs. She still wore silk stockings; deft fingers removed them. She still wore panties; they drifted away next. She moved and writhed to every clever stroke of his fingers. The kiss broke apart as she gulped greedily for breath. She was lost, gazing into eyes so black they drew her into them. Loving him, needing him.

'Do we stop?'

Do we stop…? she repeated dizzily, and tried to focus for the first time. His cheekbones stood out on a face taut with passion. His mouth wore the swollen bloom of desire gone wild. His beautiful bronzed body lay half across her and a hand was gently circling her navel.

'To continue means you accept my intentions.'

Intentions? Each time he spoke she had to work hard to grasp the words. 'Do you want to stop?' Long lashes blinked him a bemused look.

He touched his tongue to her lower lip. 'No,' he said.

'Then why ask?'

He smiled an odd smile, and used that tongue to circle the full pulsing beauty of her whole mouth. 'So be it,' he said.

She mimicked the stirring manoeuvre with an impulsiveness that for some unfathomable reason flung him over the edge. Passion roared like a lion, and the whole thing became a hot and seething whirl. He closed his mouth over one of her breasts, nipped her nipple with his teeth. As she drew in a sharp breath he sucked and played and tormented, with his mouth, with his hands. Then, with the glide of long fingers down the length of her, he descended into the cloud of gold at the apex of her thighs.

Pleasure became a greedy animal. Where he touched, she yearned for more. Her fingers dug and scraped and moulded rippling, trembling, slick male muscle. The whole thing grew like a mushroom, building pleasure on pleasure, and it made it all so much more exciting to know his breathing was ragged, that his heart was thumping madly and his body throbbing with a need as acute as her own.

I shouldn't be doing this. One single brief glimpse at sanity attempted to spoil it. She released a small whimper of distress. Then he was invading the soft tissue of her femininity with the touch of a master, and the door slammed on sanity, along with her ability to control anything, because she was flying, or as near as, her fingers clutching at him as she gasped out his name and begged him never to stop.

The ragged sound of his breathing filled her ears; the heat of his breath moistened her face. He moved over her, hair-roughened thighs parting her smooth ones. A hand slid beneath her hips to bring them towards him and she felt the first probe of his entry, then felt another set of fingers coil into her hair. He lifted her head from the bed, bringing her eyes flying open. Black heat blazed a path of fire right through her—compulsive, compelling, it warned of what was to come. Then he made that single surging thrust at the same moment his mouth smothered her cry.

It was possession in its fullest meaning. He moved, and she responded with pleasure-wracked sounds he claimed for himself. Each thrust sent him deeper, each withdrawal set her quivering in pleasurable response, each slide of damp flesh became an exquisite torment that heightened everything. When he increased the rhythm she just hung on and let him conduct the whole concert, and her imagination helped him by offering up picture flashes of pale skin against dark skin, slender white limbs clinging to majestic bronze. Darkness and sunlight became one glorious entity. He drove her into its seething depths then snapped the last thread of her control with a kiss that claimed every gasp and quiver as they came together as lost-souls in a black cavern that held back everything but the pin-sharp song of ecstasy.

He was lying beside her with his chest still heaving out the last throes of his own fulfilment. A brown hand covered his eyes. Melanie didn't move—couldn't. When she eventually managed to open her eyes it was to the grey day pouring into the bedroom and the chill that was already settling on her flesh. The ivory and blue room was about as cold a place as anyone could wish to enjoy a soulless tumble upon a strange bed. The slack-limbed languid aftermath was being replaced with reality, the dawning sense of horror, the flaying sense of dismay. What had she done—what had *they* done?

She wanted to die here, she decided. She just wanted to close her eyes and die rather than face what had to come next.

The truth. The cold, dark hollowness of truth. She'd expected him to seek revenge in one form or other, but she had not expected anything like this.

'I hate you,' she whispered as her mouth began to wobble.

He stopped breathing. The hand left his face.

'You did this on purpose. You meant to shatter me.' On a flood of tears she scrambled from the bed.

'In case you may not have noticed, I shattered too,' he fed after her quietly.

'That's different.' She began picking up her clothing. Every move, every grasp of her fingers shook with the agony of her distress. 'You're a man. You're allowed to behave like that.'

'Like what?'

'Animal!' she choked, searching the floor for her panties and not seeing them anywhere. Her cheeks were hot, yet her flesh felt so cold it was almost numb. 'Y-you look at me and see a western woman. Cheap to buy and easy to have!' she threw at him in shaken bitterness. 'You did this the last time. Y-you wanted and you took, then despised me for letting you!'

'I despised you for going from my arms into the arms of your cousin.'

'*Step*-cousin!' she corrected. 'And I am not going to discuss that with you!'

'Why not?' In a single lithe movement he snaked off the bed and came to stand over her. Naked, bold, so forcefully male, she almost sank beneath the swimming tide of her own response.

'Because you had your chance to listen eight years ago and decided it wasn't worth the effort.' Clutching her clothes to her front, she began looking wildly around her. 'Now hell will freeze over before I will defend myself to you—! Where's the bathroom?'

'Wait a minute—'

'No!' She swerved away from his reaching hands.

'Don't touch me—ever again!' The breakdown into tears was gaining momentum and she needed to get out before it happened. 'I adored you,' she whispered painfully. 'You know that I did. Y-you thought it a great hoot to relieve the besotted innocent of her virginity.'

'Hoot?' he repeated. His voice shook.

She made the mistake of looking at him.

He was laughing at her! It was the final humiliation. She turned and ran for the nearest door, found herself standing in a long wide hallway with a pale wood floor and walls painted pale blue. Where to now? Which door next? she asked herself frantically. Any door, she decided, and sped across the hall's width to the nearest one, opened it, fell inside, then closed it behind her.

It was a blue and ivory bathroom. She could not believe her one bit of good luck. With fumbling fingers she pulled her skirt up over her hips and fastened the zip. No bra, she realised, no stockings nor panties. The stretchy black top covered her naked breasts. Her nipples stung as the fabric slid across them; sparks of awareness set her teeth on edge. She pulled on the jacket and tugged it ruthlessly across her front. Then she turned to leave, caught sight of herself in a mirror and was suddenly left suspended by what she saw. Her eyes were so dark she could see no hint of gold anywhere; her mouth was swollen and pulsing and red. Her hair needing brushing. She looked wild and wanton. Cheap and easy! One kiss and you fall on him, she accused that hateful face.

Now she had a son to go home to and face, knowing what she had been doing here with his father. Nausea leapt to her throat. She spun, wondering dizzily where her bag had gone. She decided it didn't matter; she could walk home if necessary—anything so long as she could get out of here!

She tugged the door open to find him standing there waiting for her. He'd pulled on a robe, a dark blue thing that covered hardly anything. A blanket of awareness attacked each sensitised erogenous zone. 'Get out of my way,' she said through clenched teeth.

'You are not going anywhere.' A big shoulder made contact with the door frame. 'We agreed terms.'

'Terms?' She blinked. Narrowed eyes held hers with a warning glint. In a vague part of her mind she remembered words being spoken. 'Accept my intentions,' and, 'So be it.' Then he'd licked her mouth and—

'Oh, dear God,' she breathed.

'You remember?' he mocked. 'Well, that makes it easier.'

'I want to go home.' She was pale now; she could actually feel her skin turning cold and thin.

'Later,' he agreed, and a hand came out. 'Don't you want to put these on?'

He held her stockings, her bra and her panties, flimsy pieces of black silk and lace threaded through long, very male fingers that gave shamelessness a whole new edge.

But Rafiq hadn't finished with her yet—not by a long way. 'I have no objection to you choosing a ring without these on, you understand.' His dark-toned voice was remorseless. 'In fact I think it would be rather excitingly decadent to know that only you and I know you wear nothing beneath that smart suit. But the stockings, maybe, to protect your legs from the cold weather?'

'Ring?' she repeated. 'You were serious about the ring?'

Big and dark, lean and hard, he wore the face of an Arabian warlord in no mood for compromise. 'I was serious about everything,' he confirmed with silken emphasis. 'My possession of your body, the ring—my son. We will greet him as a single unit, marry with him at our side, and become a family.'

A family eight years too late. Some family, Melanie thought as the whole wretched debacle came tumbling down upon her head. Her legs went weak and she turned to lean against the inner edge of the door frame. Determined not to cry, she closed her eyes and covered her mouth with a hand.

Watching her lose the will to fight him had the odd effect of tearing at the seams of his heart. On a sigh that rid him of mockery, he tossed the scraps of silk aside. 'I do not think you cheap and easy,' he uttered grimly. 'If anything I think it is I who is guilty of being both of those things,' he admitted, with just enough bite to let his bitterness show. 'But we will put the past in abeyance and speak for now. And now demands that we pool our resources, for our son's sake.'

'You haven't even met him yet, and you're planning his life for him.'

'But I *know* him,' he declared. 'I know what it feels like to have only one parent. What it can do to his head to know that the other parent does not seem to care if he lives or he dies. I have been there before him.' It was tense, tight statement of grim factuality. 'He bleeds inside. He will bleed no longer.'

'William loved him.'

If she'd meant to hurt by saying that, then she'd succeeded. Rafiq stiffened away from the door frame. 'My half-brother, Hassan, loves me without question. But he could not be the mother I never met or fill the hole in my heart left by her.'

With that he turned and walked back into the bedroom, not liking how much of himself he had just revealed and liking even less the way that Melanie followed him when he now wished to be alone.

A familiar feeling, he noted with a tense flexing of his shoulders.

'Who was she?'

The question placed a bitter taste in his mouth. 'A Frenchwoman—Parisian,' he drawled with bite. 'Very dark, very beautiful, very much out to catch herself a rich Arab with the oldest tricks known to man.' He turned to look at her and saw a different kind of beauty standing in his bedroom doorway. A soft golden beauty—but the same flawed beauty nonetheless.

Okay, he argued with himself as he moved over to the bank of wardrobes that filled one wall. So Melanie had not blackmailed him with the child they'd made together—still was not doing that, he was forced to concede since it was he who was using the blackmail here. But she had seen her chance of marrying wealth and had been prepared to forfeit her childhood sweetheart for it.

Shame that he'd had to discover her duplicity, he thought angrily. Shame he had not married her anyway on a desire to punish her for the rest of her life. At least he would have known his child then, would have seen him grow big in her womb as Hassan was seeing his child grow. He would have been there at his son's birth, and would have loved him so much he would never have needed to know those bleak, dark little moments in life when rejection could tear at the soul.

'When she discovered that my father was already married, and his wife pregnant, she was not pleased.'

'I don't blame her,' Melanie responded. 'It sounds to me as if your father deserved the blame. He was playing with her, obviously.'

'True.' A glimpse of a hard smile touched his mouth as he pulled a clean shirt from a hanger. 'He was young, he was arrogant and unforgivably self-seeking. But when my mother decided to cut her losses and have an abortion he showed a different side to his nature by talking her out of it—or should I say that his money did the talking?' he offered cynically as he placed the shirt on the bed. 'It matters not.' He shrugged. 'She died giving birth to me.'

'I'm sorry,' Melanie murmured.

'Don't be.' The clean shirt was followed by a clean dark suit, still wrapped in a tailor's suit bag. 'The deal was that she hand me over to my father the moment it was legally possible to do so.'

'And you think that decision denies her the right to have

anyone feel sorry at her passing? That's mean and shallow, Rafiq.' He froze in the act of selecting fresh underwear. 'For all you know she might have changed her mind about you. It happens all the time. How can you condemn someone who was never given the chance to offer an opinion?'

He turned on her. 'As I was offered that chance with my child?'

She blinked, then lowered guilty eyes from him. For some reason it infuriated him to see her do that! He covered the distance between them in a few angry strides, then used his hand to capture her chin and make her to look at him. 'Yes,' he hissed at what he saw there. 'We come full circle, my unforgiving Melanie. We reach the point where this truly began. You denied me my chance just as I deny my mother her chance. It makes us two of a pair, does it not?'

'I'm giving you your chance now.' Reaching up she grasped his wrist in a useless effort to pull his hand away. 'But it doesn't have to come with a ring attached to it!'

'Yes, it does,' he insisted. 'Because my son will not remain a bastard. My son will be surrounded with love on all sides! *My* son will not be put at risk of you marrying another man who can treat him as a second-class member of his family!'

Her beautiful eyes darkened in horror. 'Who did that to you?'

He let go. 'It is of no matter.' And turned away again, cursing his own stupid mouth!

'Rafiq…' She touched his arm with sympathy.

Sympathy! The bubbling black mass of old hurts came thundering up to the surface. He turned back, knew he was losing it—*knew it* and could not stop it! 'Get out!' he breathed. 'Get out of here, Melanie, while you still can!'

What she did was step closer and wrap her arms around him like a mother would—like *she* would do with his son! 'I'm sorry,' she was saying. 'I'm sorry. I didn't know…'

He gripped her arms and tried to prise her free; he

needed to put a safe distance between them or he did not know what he would do! But she held on, lifted her face, lifted eyes that understood when he did not want anyone to understand!

'I am dangerous,' he grated. It was his final warning.

She reached up and kissed him. Blackness turned molten, molten spun itself into something else. She was amazing, fearless—foolish! She had to be to still be here when anyone with eyes must know he was about to slake all this emotion in the only way he knew how!

He caught that mouth with a kiss that blazed. He picked her up and pressed her back against the wall. Her skirt rose above her hips as he parted her legs and wrapped them around him. He entered her with no preliminary at all.

Bright fireballs of sensation propelled themselves at her senses; she clung to his shoulders and his mouth. It was all so intense that she barely noticed when he ejected into her with the shuddering groans of a man lost in hell. When it was over her feet slithered like melted wax onto the hard wood flooring. Shocked and dazed, and still caught by the pulsing aftermath of her own shimmering climax, she stared blindly at his chest, where damp whorls of black hair curled around his gaping robe.

Then once again the horror of reality hit: the knowledge that she could be so primitive! She choked on a sob as a stream of Arabic flooded over her, then hoarse thick English words of apology, of remorse and self-whipping disgust and disgrace as he picked her up in his arms and carried her out of the bedroom and down the hall.

Safety came with the neatness of a sitting room, apparently. He set her down in a low soft leather armchair, then muttered something she did not catch before striding away. A doorbell rang; he must have gone to answer it because she heard the sound of voices talking, then nothing until he came to squat down beside her and offered a glass to her trembling mouth. It was brandy; it burned as she swallowed. He took a gulp himself.

'I don't know what to say to you,' he pushed out thickly.

Her lashes flickered downwards as she made herself look into his face. He was as white as the chair she was sitting on, guilt-riddled and appalled with himself.

'I'll marry you,' she whispered. 'I'll marry you.'

'Why?' He couldn't have sounded more stunned if he'd tried.

Tears filled her eyes. It was all so—*basic!* She wanted him again so very badly it burned like a wound inside! He filled her with a thousand contradictions. Anger, hurt, resentment, confusion—desire! He ran cold, then hot, was ruthlessly hard and tough, yet so very vulnerable it almost broke her heart.

And then they came—the words that really mattered. She was still in love him, even after all these years and all the heartache and pain and the sense of betrayal. She still loved him no matter what or why. Realising that hurt more than anything else did. She couldn't tell him—would *never* tell him.

'Robbie needs you,' she said.

Robbie needs you. Once again they'd arrived back at the beginning. A different beginning in an ever-confusing spiral of beginnings.

He stood up. It was a withdrawal in many ways. 'Yes,' he said. 'Of course. I will go and dress. You may safely use the bathroom to—tidy yourself before we leave.'

CHAPTER SIX

His suit was a dark blue, almost black, in colour, the fabric an exquisite weave of silk. His shirt was white, his tie blue, and the whole ensemble blended perfectly with the man he had turned himself into.

Cleanly shaven face; neatly combed hair; raven eyelashes keeping a permanent guard over his eyes, and his mouth a beautifully defined example of sombre elegance. Melanie had to bite hard into her bottom lip so as not to say a word. If he'd dressed like this to put Robbie at his ease with him then he could not have got it more wrong. Her son was more likely to stand in awe than feel at ease. Rafiq was the ice man, a man who belonged in a palace built of glass, steel and marble.

She shivered and fiddled with the ring on her finger. It was made of gold and bright, flawless sparkling diamonds. She had chosen it from a luscious selection set on a black velvet tray in the privacy of his sitting room. Between her running for cover in the bathroom and their confrontation across its threshold he had called up a top London jeweller and had had them bring a selection to his apartment.

It was money wielding its awesome power. She shivered again; he shifted tensely and sent her a sharp look that scoured the skin from the part of her profile he could see. Sitting next to each other in this car was the closest they'd been to each other since he'd fed her the brandy. No eye contact nor body contact, words spoken as if through a glass wall. Why? Because they'd delved into a dark place they knew they should never have visited. It had exposed too much of an inner core that most preferred to keep hidden away.

Now here they were, driving towards her home where another ordeal was about to be enacted. Melanie tried to swallow and found that she couldn't. From the corner of her eye she caught sight of his hand where it rested on his thigh. The long fingers moved ever so slightly, but she could almost taste the tension that forced them to make that minuscule jerk. She dared a quick glance up from beneath her lashes and almost shattered on impact with the hard profile of a cold and aloof Arabian male: his long thin nose; his curling black eyelashes hovering against the firm glossy texture of his olive-toned skin; his jaw line taut and rock-like, the set of his mouth implacable and flat. If she superimposed Arab clothes over the suit she could be looking at the Arabian prince he was in everything but name.

But that memory belonged to another time, and it did nothing for her nerves to remember it now. Daunting as he was in his western sophistication, she preferred it to that other man she had met only once, when he'd torn her apart with his contempt.

This time she managed to contain the shiver. 'Robbie might mention your father,' she heard herself say as thoughts of his ruthless Arab side led her onto other things.

The dark head turned with frightening precision; eyes too dark to read fixed on her face. 'He knows about my father?'

It was too quietly and too smoothly spoken. Melanie tried that swallow again. 'W-William liked to keep him informed ab-about your country,' she explained. 'Your father's poor health is reported in the press occasionally, and a party six months ago was given quite a lot of coverage. A thirty-year anniversary?' she prompted.

He nodded. So did she, then dragged her eyes away to look down at the ring again. 'Robbie decided that your father's ill health m-must have kept you at home with him. H-he worries about things like that, so it suited him to give you that particular reason why you didn't come to London.'

The hand resting on his thigh gave that telling minuscule twitch once more. 'Without William Portreath's money, would you ever have told me about him?'

It wasn't harsh but it was coldly accusing. 'Robbie only started asking questions about you a year ago. He never asked to see you, but if he had done I'd like to think I would have done something about it.'

'You'd like to think?' he repeated.

'I had to protect both him and myself,' she reiterated.

'From me?'

'From this!' she cried, shattering the wall between them with a spectacular eruption, blasting away all of this nice polite civility. 'Look at what you've already done, Rafiq! Even with William's money as my so-called safeguard. I've been packed up and taken over! You did it before. You packed me up and took me over, then dropped me like a brick when I didn't come up to your high expectations!'

'You are twisting the truth.'

'No, I'm not.' Trying to make the eruption subside again was impossible. The bubble had burst and she suddenly didn't know what she was doing, sitting here next to him travelling towards calamity at what felt like the speed of light. 'If Robbie can't meet those same high expectations does he get dropped?' she pushed out thickly. 'Do you truly think I believe I am doing the right thing bringing you into his life? Because I don't! You're so hard and tough and unpredictable.' She sat upright on a raw flick of tension. 'You blow hot, then icy cold. I can't tell what you're going to do next, and I'm frightened I've made a huge error of judgement here. I feel like I'm playing Russian roulette with a child's life!'

'I will not drop him!' he raked at her. 'Nor you, for that matter,' he added with a lofty promise that aimed to put all the emotion back under wraps but didn't quiet make it. 'And if you still feel this way, why am I here at all?' he demanded, and brought the whole thing toppling down again.

Melanie looked down at her tightly clenched hands, then out of the car window while her chest grew tight on words she did not want to speak.

But time was beginning to run out. 'William's death had a profound effect on Robbie,' she told him. 'He suddenly realised that without William he had only me to take care of him. So he worries that I—'

'Might die too and leave him with no one.' Rafiq took over in a deep voice so drenched in bleak understanding that she glanced sharply at him.

He was sitting there with the same carved profile, but his eyes had come alive, burning with a personal knowledge that brought into hard focus the kind of childhood he'd experienced as a motherless son—a second son and an illegitimate one at that.

'Y-you had your brother,' she reminded him.

His tight smile mocked the remark. 'Hassan is six months older than I am. Every time his mother looked at me she saw the bitter proof of her husband's infidelity while she was heavily pregnant. Do you think she didn't yearn for the day when she could toss me out of her household? In the end she died before she could achieve her dearest wish, but as a child I learned to appreciate the vulnerability of my situation.'

'I'm sorry. I didn't know.'

'How could you?' He shrugged. 'These are not the kind of memories a man usually shares with other people.'

Not even with the woman he professed to love? If he had been a bit more open with her eight years ago maybe she would have stood a chance at understanding what had made him the man he was, and dealt with the situation of Robbie differently.

'So, he worries?' Rafiq prompted.

She nodded. 'He has nightmares about it,' she confessed, and watched in thick-throated distress as he turned his head so she could see those dark knowing eyes. 'He worries himself sick if I so much as sneeze. As I've been saying from the start, he—'

'Needs me,' Rafiq finished. 'As back-up,' he added.

It sounded so very cold put like that, but— 'Yes,' she confirmed.

'And if I had not come through with this back-up?'

She looked away and did not answer. But, being the man he was, he had already worked out what her alternatives were going to be. His hand snaked out to catch her chin, then he made her to look back at him. Hard eyes glinted into her eyes. 'As far as my son and his mother are concerned I will not be walking away,' he vowed very clearly. 'So you may put away any other options, Melanie. For the ring on your finger will be joined by another, and you will not need to look elsewhere for anything—understand?'

Yes. She nodded and let her eyelashes flutter onto her cheeks so he couldn't read her thoughts. Because she was beginning to understand an awful lot of things, and none of them helped her to feel less anxious about the situation. With every word he uttered, Rafiq was revealing an affinity with his son that promised to grow into a bond like no other. Who would become the expendable link then? She would, and on realising it she began to appreciate what it meant to feel so frighteningly vulnerable.

The car pulled up outside her house. Melanie was never so relieved for an excuse to escape. She went to pull her chin free of his fingers, but he held on until she surrendered and looked back up at him. The glow in his eyes was skin-piercingly covetous. It pricked at just about every nerve-end she possessed. The sexual pull was stunning; the emotional one threatened to strip her bare. Sparks flew; her breathing snagged; for a few blind seconds she had to fight the urge to turn her mouth into those cool fingers and say something calamitous like, I still love you, Rafiq.

She wanted to run and Rafiq didn't blame her. He could

not look at her without the sexual fallout drenching the air. The cool tips of his fingers slid against skin like fine satin, the inner recesses of his mouth sprang into life with a need to taste what he could feel. A driving compulsion to lean down and take what was throbbing in the atmosphere held him motionless, because he dared not even breathe in case he gave in to its magnetic pull.

He had revealed the absolute worst of himself to her today, yet she was still sitting here looking at him through those hungry eyes. Why was that? he asked himself. She was wearing his ring and was prepared to marry him when she had to know his arguments for marriage were a bluff, and that she possessed the resources to turn her back on him if she so pleased.

Was she doing this for their son? A son who had not even looked upon his father's face and who, when he did, might well decide he didn't like what he saw! What then— what did Melanie do then?

He removed his fingers and looked away from her, and heard her feather out a shaky breath. His driver opened the door for her. She scrambled out of the car and hurried up the path to fumble the key into the lock of her front door. The black suit skimmed her slender figure; her pale hair swung around her slender nape. His heart gave a tug. It was fear. He grabbed it and crushed it down again.

It had stopped raining but the air was cold and damp. As he stepped out of the car he felt it seep into his bones and had a sudden wish to be at home, standing beneath the relentless heat of the desert sun.

But first he had a son to meet and a relationship to build. His heart gave a different kind of tug, and he grimaced as he turned to dismiss his driver. Then he swung back to look at the house into which Melanie had already disappeared. The car moved away as he walked up the path. As he walked inside the house seemed to stir, like a sleeping monster awakening from a long dark slumber as its senses picked up on the scent of threat.

Threat to whom? To Melanie or his son? Was it William Portreath's ghost Rafiq could sense stirring in the shadows, watching Rafiq infiltrate his domain so he could see for himself if he was a worthy successor? He gave himself a mental shake. He wasn't usually prone to such superstitious nonsense, he grimly mocked himself.

A sound came from the living room and he stepped into it to find Melanie on her knees in front of the fire, putting a light to the logs neatly aligned in the grate. Flames leaped to life and she was on her feet, moving round the room lighting faded old lamps, plumping faded old cushions. 'Make yourself at home,' she invited. 'I need to go and change before— The fire should be okay, and I've switched on the central heating system so the house will heat up pretty quickly.'

For a man who had never walked into any of his many homes needing to think about what kept it heated—or cool, for that matter—Rafiq viewed all this brisk domesticity through vaguely shocked eyes. She disappeared into the hallway. He listened to her light footsteps as she ran up the stairs, and heard a door open and close. A few minutes later the clock on the mantelpiece chimed the half-hour. It was instinctive when he hitched back a snowy white shirt cuff to check the time on his state-of-the-art satellite-controlled wrist-watch and grimaced when he discovered that the old wooden-cased clock was accurate almost to the second.

Three-thirty, Melanie noted. That left them with ten short minutes before Robbie arrived back from school, and she tried not to predict what was going to happen as she scrambled out of her suit and into jeans and a pale blue sweater, then brushed her hair while avoiding any contact with a mirror because—

A ball of heat rolled in her stomach, then sank to the apex at her thighs. She caught her breath, then just stood there staring at the old-fashioned roses on the wallpaper while her head decided to play her some flashbacks from the last few hours just to make the feeling worse.

Oh, she'd behaved like an absolute wanton. What must he be thinking about her?

He—Rafiq ben Jusef Al Alain Al-Qadim. She gave him his name and was immediately hit with his naked image. Big, dark, muscular and sleek, with curling black hair following the contours of his long torso from his wide chest like an arrowhead pointing the way to the enthralling eminence of his, of his—

No. She blinked the image away, eyelashes fluttering with a terrible reluctance to let the image fade, which brought a flush to her cheeks as she slid her feet into a pair of lightweight flat shoes and tried very hard to concentrate her mind on what lay ahead of them instead of what lay behind.

She came down the stairs to the sound of a car engine idling outside the front gate. A door slammed; there was a child's shout of 'See you!' and her whole body froze on a moment's stark panic of what was about to happen.

The door was on the latch. She always made sure it was left on the latch so that Robbie could let himself in. His bag arrived first, swinging in through the door to land on the polished wood floor before he propelled himself inside. His tie was flying, as usual, his shirt collar curled up towards his chin.

'Hi,' he said, seeing her standing there as he closed the door behind him.

'Hi, yourself.' Her heart dipped and dived as she made herself walk forward on legs that felt hollow. 'Have you had a nice day today?'

'We've been making Christmas cards,' he informed her as she went down on her haunches in front of him. 'Mrs Dukes is going to print lots of copies so we can send them to our friends.'

'Well, that sounds like a good idea.' She smiled, or tried

to, while anxiously straightening his shirt collar and running shaky fingers through his ruffled hair.

'What are you doing that for?' Robbie frowned at her. 'I'm going to get changed in a minute.'

'Because I have a surprise for you,' she told him, feeling her tension hit its highest point, and feeling yet more tension coming at her in waves from inside the living room. She wondered what Rafiq was thinking, feeling—*doing*!

'A surprise?' Robbie prompted.

'Yes.' She smiled and straightened, then took hold of his hand. 'A really marvellous surprise. Come and see.'

With that she led him towards the living room, heart in her mouth as she brought him to a halt in the open doorway. She felt Robbie look up, felt him stiffen, then felt her own deep sinking sensation as she looked up into Rafiq's carved face. He was still standing where she had left him in the middle of the room, with the firelight flickering behind him. The air crashed with tension. It was sheer motherly instinct that made her swing her son to stand in front of her with his back to her, her arms wrapping themselves around him so she could feel his little heart pounding like a hammer drill.

'Rafiq, th-this is Robbie.' She made that first stammering introduction.

'Robbie,' she murmured gently to her son, 'this is—'

'My daddy,' the little boy said.

No one could have predicted he was going to say that. Melanie wasn't even aware how he knew what his father looked like; Rafiq just looked shell-shocked.

'I saw you in a picture William showed to me,' Robbie enlightened them. 'You were in Egypt with a lady, but you weren't dressed like that, though.' He frowned at the smart Italian suit. 'You had Arab clothes on and the lady had on a red frilly dress.'

As her son built a host of vivid pictures in his mother's head he also began slipping through her fingers, drawn towards Rafiq as if he'd known him since birth and had simply been waiting for him to come. Through eyes gone glassy with tears and a heart almost too swollen to manage to beat, she watched Rafiq observe with bottomless black fascination as his son approached him with his head tipped back so his eyes could maintain contact with his.

Move! Melanie wanted to shout at him. Make a response! Can't you see how brave he is being, coming to you like this? As if she'd shrieked the words out loud the stiffness faded from Rafiq's body and he lowered his big frame to his son's level.

'Hello,' he murmured rustily.

'Hello,' Robbie replied gravely. Black eyes searched black eyes for a few seconds. Then Robbie made his next courageous move and lifted up a hand and offered it to his father. Rafiq took it. Melanie watched through her tears as his large hand closed around her son's tiny one.

It was the first touch, first contact. She saw Rafiq's mouth move in response to it, then saw no more as tears blurred the rest of the tableau, and the silence throbbing all around them threatened to suffocate all three.

Then Robbie spoke again. 'Can you ride a camel?'

A camel, Melanie repeated to herself numbly as she listened to Rafiq's thickened reply. 'Yes.'

'William said you would know how. William said...'

She took the coward's way out, turned and made a dash for the kitchen, where she gave her legs permission to fold and slid into a huddle on the floor in a corner. She pressed her face into her knees, covered her ears with her hands and waited in trembling agony for the emotions trampling through her to subside.

The telephone began to ring, cutting through everything like an unwelcome intruder. She leaped up, wiped her eyes with trembling fingers, and made herself answer it.

It was Sophia, ringing to tell her she had decided to stay the weekend in Manchester with friends. 'How's it going?' she asked.

'Robbie is with his father in the other room,' she announced huskily.

'So he remembered to turn up.' Sophia had called Melanie every day to check on progress and had become more hostile with every day that Rafiq hadn't put in an appearance. 'If he hurts that boy, I'll—'

'They came together like long-lost friends!' Melanie said with a choke. 'Give them both a few minutes and they will have me all trussed up and labelled as the bad guy for keeping them apart!'

'Then don't let them do it,' Sophia said firmly. 'You know why you kept Robbie a secret from him. Just keep on reminding yourself that the rat dumped you without cause, on the hearsay of some very twisted people, and then left you alone and damn near destitute to carry his can of oats!'

His can of oats. Melanie couldn't help it; she laughed. 'Thanks,' she murmured.

'Don't mention it,' Sophia dismissed. 'I can still remember what you looked like when you turned up on William's doorstep as fat as a pig and looking like the original bag lady. Homeless, loveless and still trying to get a line of communication through to that arrogant fool sitting comfortably on his billions.'

'He doesn't know that.'

'Well, *tell* him!'

'No.' The stubborn lip protruded. 'That belongs in the past and I am determined to concentrate only on the future.' She paused, then decided to get the really bad news over with. 'We—we're getting married,' she added reluctantly.

'*What—?*'

Melanie winced. 'We decided it was the best thing for everyone. Robbie needs him—even you agree with that, Sophia! And marriage seems to be the best way to give him the security he—'

'Are you mad?' her friend shrieked. 'I'm coming home,' she decided.

'No!' Melanie cried. 'Don't do that, Sophia! I know what I'm doing, I—'

'You're a babe in arms when it comes to men, is what you are, Melanie Portreath!' the other woman derided. 'Have you stopped for one minute to think what his motives are for suggesting such a wicked thing?'

Oh, yes, Melanie thought, she'd stopped to think. The word HOT lit itself up in block capitals, followed by the word SEX!

'He will rush you to his desert hideout and lock you away there while he waltzes off with your son! It's the way they do things over there! Get behind me, woman, and all that!'

'He isn't like that,' she said, agitatedly twisting the ring on her finger.

'*All* men are like that if they think they can get away with it!'

'You don't know him—'

'Neither do you! You just slept with him once—'

Twice, Melanie silently corrected, then closed her eyes and thought—three times if you counted the last feverish grappling.

'Then he took off, with your virginity etched on his belt,' Sophia was saying, with no knowledge that Melanie had just taken off to a place she knew she should not be revisiting. 'And left *you* behind with the word *slut* etched on to your blasted forehead!'

Melanie blinked. Sophia was right. She had walked around for years thinking that word was branded on her brow. She hadn't dared trust herself with another man just in case he believed it and treated her the same way that Rafiq had done.

'Do me a favour, Melanie, and don't do anything stupid until I get back,' Sophia said urgently. 'Then we will grab your lawyer and sit down to talk through all of this.'

'Okay.' It made a lot of sense—more sense than she had been making all day, for that matter. 'But don't cut short your weekend or I won't forgive you!'

The call ended with Sophia reluctantly agreeing to wait until Monday before she began her crusade to save Melanie from a fate worse than death. Melanie put the telephone back on its rest, feeling a whole lot better for having had Sophia talk stubborn strength back into her.

It lasted only as long as it took her to prepare Robbie's favourite meal of pasta with tuna then to go in search of the two of them. She found them in William's study, and the moment she stepped through the door her new-found strength collapsed like a house of cards.

The room itself said everything about the man who had spent most of his life in it. The walls were lined with books, the furniture was so old it was threadbare. The fire wasn't lit and the two high-wing-backed chairs that flanked the fireplace looked as if they had been there for centuries. There was a chill in the air because the room was so rarely used these days, but someone had closed the heavy velvet curtains across the window and had switched on the faded table-lamps.

William's big old desk stood in the window. Robbie had pulled a chair up to it to kneel on while Rafiq stood beside him. Both of them had lost their jackets, both dark heads were close as they pored over the huge map that had been spread out across the top of the desk. Robbie was using an elbow to support his chin, Rafiq the flat of a hand as he listened to his son tell him all about the Arabian state of Rahman as if he had lived most of his life there.

'William said the river here keeps the valley fertile. And the mountains have snow on them in the winter,' Robbie was explaining casually. 'He said that you can walk for six days without seeing anything but sand, and that your daddy built this huge place—here—for the camel trains to use when they need to take a rest.'

His finger was pointing knowledgeably, but Rafiq

wasn't watching it. He was watching his son. The light from the desk lamp caught both sets of features, one young and smooth and contentedly serious, the other carved like wood to represent total infatuation.

'William said you have the biggest oasis in the country. Is that true?' He looked up, big brown eyes fixing on their older matching pair.

'It belongs to my father.' Rafiq nodded. 'It is called the Al-Qadim Oasis. My—home is there.'

'Yes.' The boy looked away again, graver now, worried a little. 'William said that your daddy is poorly. Is he feeling better? Is that why you've come to visit me?'

'I came because—yes…' Rafiq paused, then answered, 'he is a little better.'

'Good.' Robbie nodded. 'William was poorly for a long time before he— Shall we look at the photographs now?'

'How about some supper first?' Melanie inserted, trying hard to keep the thickening tears from sounding in her voice.

Both looked up; both straightened. One smiled at her; the other didn't. 'Hi,' Robbie said. 'I was just telling my daddy about Rahman.'

My daddy clutched at a tender spot inside her. 'That's nice.' She tried a smile but couldn't quite pull it off. 'But it's getting late. Why don't you go and get washed and changed now? It's your favourite for supper.'

'Tuna? Oh, great!' At once he was her little boy again, all beaming smiles and bouncing energy that had him leaping from the chair to land neatly on the faded carpet. He came towards her with a jaunty little stride—then stopped, the smile fading from his face as he turned to look at Rafiq. 'You won't go while I'm upstairs, will you?' he said cautiously.

'No, I won't go,' Rafiq promised him.

'Great,' Robbie said again, then grinned widely. 'Great!' he repeated, and was running out of the room, leaving two adults with a fallout he would never understand in a million years.

The moment they were alone Rafiq turned his back on her, broad shoulders like rods as he stared down at the map. 'I will never forgive you for this,' he breathed harshly.

'Won't forgive me for what?' she took the challenge head-on.

'*This!*' he rasped, waving a hand across the spread map. 'He knows more about Rahman than I know about it! He can plot a track across the desert from one of my homes to another!' he stated harshly. 'And he has learned it all from another man!'

'William—'

'Yes, *William!*' he incised, then gave his big shoulders a shrug, as if to rid them of whatever it was that was sitting on them. 'I think it is time you told me about William Portreath,' he demanded tightly.

Tension spun through every tight syllable, bitterness and anger and—yes, Melanie realised there was a burning jealousy for the love and affection Robbie felt for William.

CHAPTER SEVEN

RAFIQ did not know what he was feeling. He tried grabbing in a lungful of air in effort to control himself, but he was way past the point of controlling anything. The last hour had been heaven and hell wrapped in one package. He had never felt such instant attachment to another human being, and all that person could talk about was William Portreath.

He turned to glare at Melanie. She was standing in the doorway looking wary and stubborn, and it was clear she did not want to have this kind of discussion with him.

'Please,' he ground out from his chest like the rattle of a pistol.

With a little jerk she swung the door almost shut behind her, her fingers still clutching at the handle and her shoulders straight and tense.

'Okay,' she agreed reluctantly. 'What is it that you want to know?

His teeth gritted at the reluctance, and his chest clenched at the rebellious expression on her beautiful face. But he had a right to know, dammit! 'Exactly what was William Portreath to you?'

'If you'd read my papers you would know what he was,' she returned. 'William was my great-uncle on my mother's side. He made his fortune travelling the world as a diamond merchant before coming back to England to retire.'

Her left hand appeared from behind her back and she glanced down at the diamond ring circling her finger. So did Rafiq, and he felt his skin prickle when he remembered the safety deposit box listed in her assets; it was packed full of diamonds that could probably kill the sparkle in the ones she wore on her finger.

'You were his only beneficiary,' he said, as if that had anything to do with all this. It didn't. He was just linking one thought with another.

'I didn't know that until he'd died,' Melanie made clear. 'In fact I did not even know of William's existence until my twenty-first birthday, when a letter arrived from Randal's firm informing me that I was William's heir and he would like to meet me,' she explained. 'So I agreed to come here to see him, and found myself faced with this crabby old eccentric.' An odd little smile softened the defiance from her mouth. 'We had a fight—'

'About what?'

'William had known since the time when my parents died that I would inherit from him. He also knew that I had been sent off to live with another obscure uncle but, because he didn't want the responsibility of a child cluttering up his reclusive life, he chose to ignore my existence until I was—old enough to be sensible, as he put it.' Her mouth took on a bitter twist now. 'But he didn't get a sensible person. He got an angry one who was heavily pregnant and with no sign of a man to make her respectable.'

Rafiq flinched. 'I can do simple arithmetic.'

'William called me a few unpleasant names that you would recognise,' she said, retaliating to his bite. 'And I called him a few names in return. I went to leave. He stood up to stop me, tripped over his walking stick and would have fallen if I hadn't grabbed him. It—it was like holding frail skin and bone in my arms,' she recalled, not seeing the way Rafiq stiffened in recognition of that sentiment. 'H-he asked me to stay,' she went on. 'He was lonely. I was—in need of a roof over my head, so I stayed.'

Her accompanying shrug said, End of story. But as far as Rafiq was concerned it was only the beginning of it.

'So you allowed William Portreath to become both father to my son and a grandfather in place of my own father!'

'Am I supposed to feel guilty for allowing William to give Robbie something no one else would?'

'Yes…' He moved restlessly. 'You should be feeling as guilty as hell.'

Melanie was not impressed. 'You can say that now,' she mocked. 'But we both know you didn't feel like that eight years ago. You just walked away.'

'I did not know I was leaving a son behind.'

'You didn't want to know.'

'How can you say that? How dare you say that when you never gave me the opportunity to make that decision?'

'A decision?' she flicked back at him, and was suddenly lurching away from the door to come and stand directly in front of him. 'You think it required a *decision* as to whether you condescended to want Robbie or not? How dare you stand here and be so conceited?' she said angrily. 'How dare you be so bloody superior that you can even put up such an argument? You threw me out without a hearing!' Her golden eyes flicked the accusation at him. 'That was your decision, Rafiq. Anything at all that came after that was *my* decision! And I did not *decide* to love Robbie. I just *do* love him. Can you possibly understand the difference?'

'Jamie,' he installed into the argument. 'As a mother you love without question, no matter who is the father of your child. But a father needs to trust he *is* the father before he can dare to love! You slept with Jamie within a week of sleeping with me.' His hand flicked out to toss that claim at her. 'You cannot possibly have known, therefore, which of us was his father until the boy was born.'

'Is this leading somewhere?' she demanded coldly.

Was it? Rafiq asked himself. 'Yes,' he hissed. 'Once you knew for sure that I was Robert's father you had a moral duty to get in touch with me.'

Nothing—he received absolutely nothing back from that

final accusation. Her rebellious eyes held his steady; her mouth remained defiantly shut. She had planted her hands on hips and was taking him on as if she was easily up to his weight in a battle. Frustration attached itself to his ribs and his fingers. He wanted to reach out with those fingers and shake her into talking—and he wanted to wrap her to his aching ribs and just kiss her senseless!

He sighed, wishing he knew what it was that was actually driving him here, but he didn't. There were so many feelings trampling around inside him that he couldn't distinguish one from the other. His gaze shifted around a room that was not dissimilar to a room his father had in Rahman. He looked at the map again and saw the years he'd been robbed of by his own blind stubbornness represented on the desk, and also in the sound of his son's voice unwittingly telling him how William Portreath had attempted to give them to the child.

It hurt. This house hurt. This room, the dead man who still lingered inside it—this woman and her refusal to admit that she owed him something for what she'd taken away!

'I need to get out of here,' he decided suddenly. It was that quick, that desperate, and he just stepped around her and walked away.

As he made for the door Melanie felt the bitterness rise up and try to strangle her. 'So you still walk away from promises you make.' She slid the words deridingly after him. 'What happened to your "united we stand" speech, Rafiq?' she taunted. 'Or the promise you gave to your son that you would still be here when he comes downstairs?'

Rigid back, rigid shoulders; he went still by the door. 'I am finding it impossible to justify that for seven years my son has been deprived of his right to know a father's love,' he said harshly. 'And that William Portreath stole something from my father that did not belong to him!'

'William didn't steal anything from anyone. I did.'

He turned to look at her. Pale but still perfect, Melanie

thought painfully. Still loftily superior, but struggling with it. 'William Portreath aided and abetted you to keep my son hidden away from me!' He stated it clearly.

Melanie pulled in some air, then made herself say what she knew she didn't want to say. 'On the day Robbie was born William begged me to tell you about our son and offered me any money I might need to fight you in court,' she confessed. 'I refused.'

His eyes narrowed. 'I don't believe you.'

'I don't care what you believe,' she returned. 'I know it is the truth. This has never had anything to do with money. It was to do with a man who could walk away from his promises and never—ever—look back! Now here you are, intending to do the same thing again. Only this time you're going to break a small boy's heart instead of a stupid young woman's!'

'You never loved me,' he said, denouncing that claim. 'It was always the money! You were always only looking for a rich man to take you out of the hole you lived in!'

'And I chose you?' Melanie gasped out. 'Think back, Rafiq, and tell me who it was that did the chasing! Because I recall you virtually laying siege to me!'

'Tactics,' he said cynically. 'You played the game perfectly.'

'No.' Melanie denied that. 'If I'd been playing the tactical game I would have made you wait for sex until the ring was safely on my finger. But not me—not this gullible fool!' A shudder of self-disgust ripped through her. 'I gave you it all—just as I gave it to you again today—and if you think I am proud of myself for that, then think again, because you have a real knack for making me despise myself!'

She turned away from his stunned expression, despising herself all the more for letting fly at him. What was she trying to do here? Bury her pride completely? She lifted a hand to cover her mouth with it, caught the glitter of a diamond and with tears suddenly burning in her eyes she wrenched the ring from her finger and stepped up to hand it back to him.

The swine took it—he *took it*! 'Now you can leave,' she whispered shakily.

Footsteps suddenly sounded on the upper landing, then came clattering down the stairs. Both stopped breathing and went perfectly still. It lasted only a couple of seconds and Rafiq was the first to recover. His eyes gave a flash like lightning—the only warning Melanie received before she was being crushed in his arms. Heat drenched her body from the burn of the kiss; tension ricocheted through her muscles as she tried to fight him. In a single smooth movement he'd caught her mouth and was lifting them both out of the way from the door as their son pushed it open. Robbie just stood there, staring at the fascinating sight of his mother kissing his newly found father.

Deliberate. The whole swift, nerve-shaking move had been a deliberate one aimed to make a particular impression on their highly impressionable son. When Rafiq finally released her mouth Melanie found herself staring at the hand she had splayed out against his snow-white shirt front. Somewhere between the grab and the kiss Rafiq had also slid the ring back onto her finger. It was now sparkling at her in much the same way as her son was sparkling.

'You were kissing my mum,' Robbie accused.

'Mmm,' Rafiq agreed. 'I like kissing her, and she likes me doing it...'

Melanie's gaze jumped from the ring to his face. Those devil-black eyes were glinting down on her with lazy triumph. Deny it if you can, that mocking glint challenged. She was breathless—helpless—literally stewing in her own foolish response. And what made it all so much worse was that Rafiq knew it. He released a low, soft, throaty laugh, caught the hand wearing the ring, then swung them both to face their small witness. 'We have been talking about what to do about us,' he informed his son smoothly. 'How would you feel about us becoming a proper family, Robert?'

Robert. Melanie blinked at the *Robert* she'd only ever heard William use. Then she blinked again at her son, who was suddenly wearing a smile that lit his whole face. 'Will you come here and live with us?' Robbie demanded in breathless excitement.

Rafiq's brief moment of stillness was Melanie's only reward for the web she was allowing herself to be wrapped in. He hadn't thought as far on as *where* they were going to live. Then he said, 'Yes. Tonight, I think. What do you think?' he deferred to his star-struck son.

'Oh, yes!' Robbie exclaimed, as if he'd just had his dearest wish granted.

'Good,' Rafiq murmured. 'Then you may show me to the room in which I am to sleep…'

'Rafiq…'

Her one burst of protest was denied by a man intent on getting his own way. Lifting the hand wearing his ring to his mouth, he kissed it and murmured, 'Hush,' then gently let her go so he could turn his full attention on Robbie. His hand was offered to his son. Watching through a daze, she saw Robbie's smaller hand disappear inside it. As the long fingers closed she felt something clutch at her heart. The pair began to move out of the room, man and boy linked by their hands and a genetic influence that was so strong it hurt.

Maybe she even groaned at the recognition, she wasn't sure, but something made Robbie stop and turn his head to look at her. 'Is something the matter?' he asked frowningly.

'No, of course not.' She smiled. 'I am just trying to decide whether to eat in the kitchen or go all posh and use the dining room.'

The diversion was an inspiration. Robbie's eyes widened in dismay. 'Not the dining room, Mum!' he protested.

'It's all big and cold in there.' His hand gave a tug at his father's hand. 'We can eat in the kitchen, can't we?'

There's your choice, big man, Melanie thought cynically. The boy, the trusting hand, the kitchen and the house. The arc of his silky black lashes curled against his high cheekbones as he looked down at his son.

'The kitchen sounds perfect,' Rafiq agreed.

'Good.' Robbie beamed. 'I knew you'd want to. William liked the kitchen the very best—and this room, of course. Come on, let's go upstairs to my room. You'll like it…'

Robbie didn't see his mother wince at his mention of William. He didn't see Rafiq's fleeting glance her way before he allowed himself to be pulled towards the stairs.

Later they sat at the scrubbed kitchen table, eating pasta turned to rubber, pretending to enjoy it. Rafiq had probably never eaten in a kitchen in his life before, Melanie mused. He had probably never eaten from anything but the best bone china, nor been forced to sleep in a draughty old bedroom.

Then she took that last thought back with an inner snatch when she recalled her bedroom at the farmhouse. It had been cold and draughty. The bed had been an ancient metal-sprung affair with a deep feather mattress and a propensity to creak when they…

She got up from the table in an agitated flurry, bringing two pairs of matching eyes shooting questions her way. She ignored them, moved to the sink with her plate, then just stood there driven into remembering the man and the bed and the way he had drawn her down upon it, his dark face wearing the intensity of what had taken him over. He had touched and tutored her, had slowly brought her to a yearning pitch at which she would rather have died than drawn back from accepting him.

But the bed—the bed had creaked and groaned like a guilty accomplice. The room had been so cold he had pulled the heavy eiderdown over them, cocooning them in warmth and the soft, heaving rush of their own sensual breathing. Flesh moving against flesh, scents stirring the senses. They'd remained there throughout a whole afternoon while her uncle and Jamie had been out in the barn, and the old farmhouse had rattled against an icy storm hitting its outer walls—while another storm beneath the eiderdown had been hot and sultry.

Someone touched her shoulder. She almost jumped in the air. It was Rafiq. She jerked away. He released a small sigh and turned her to face him.

Big; his chest was big, wide and deep and beautifully masculine. Her breasts sprang to life, tightening and tingling and sending messages down to other parts of her that droned with an ache she did not want to feel.

'Where's Robbie?' she murmured, vaguely aware that they were alone in the kitchen.

'Gone to find a video I am to watch,' her son's father replied, with just a hint of huskiness that told her he was touched by his son's desire to share everything with him. 'But I wanted to take this moment to apologise for my remarks earlier. You were right: William Portreath is not to be blamed. He was a good man. He loved my son. I can only thank him for taking care of Robert as wisely as he did. It is no wonder Robert misses him.'

She nodded, unable to speak. He believed she had been standing here thinking of their argument when in reality her thoughts had been lost in a different kind of place entirely. She ought to be ashamed of herself, but oddly she wasn't. She was hot and hungry struggling not to close the two-inch gap between his chest and the tingling tips of her eager breasts.

'Y-you can't stay here. It wouldn't be right.' She managed the sensible sentence.

'The decision has been made. I do not back down on my promises.'

'To your son.' It was bitter. 'You are cynically using him to get your own way where I am concerned.'

'To both of you,' he insisted. 'And cynical I may be, but the sooner we place this relationship on a permanent footing, the sooner we can give Robert what he needs.'

'Stop calling him Robert,' she snapped out impulsively.

'It is his name,' he insisted. 'And why are you trembling?'

Melanie almost laughed out loud at the question. 'Because I think I am going to fall into a flood of tears,' she lied, instead of telling the truth—that she was longing to fall on him like a ravenous fool!

Though the tears weren't that far away, she realised. Tears and desire. What a combination. Both ate away at self-control. She tried to move away; his hands pressed her closer. Two inches became a half an inch. Her trembling became a fine shimmer. Could he feel it? Yes he could feel it; his fingertips were moving lightly against her spine, as if to encourage it.

'Please let me go now,' she said a little desperately.

'When you look at me.'

'No.' She didn't want to look at him so she turned her face and looked at the kitchen, with its old-fashioned familiarity, and wondered why he didn't look utterly out of place in here.

'Why not?' he challenged, and his voice was like a quiet rumble, vibrating all around her, husky, sexy.

Don't give in to it, she told herself, then tipped her head back, made contact with eyes like the darkest brown velvet set between ebony lashes. They drew her in as she'd known they would. They sent messages she'd already read via a body language that was threatening to pull her apart inside.

'I didn't betray you with Jamie,' she whispered.

On a growl of anger he swooped with his mouth and captured her throbbing declaration, captured and returned it to her with the furious flick of his tongue. He didn't believe her. He didn't *want* to believe her. Because to believe meant he would have to place himself so much in the wrong that his ego wouldn't cope with what that would brand him.

Bitterness welled again, scouring out the desire that had held her in his arms so long. She broke away from the kiss, moved away from his body, and turned away from the whole tempting package being sold to her.

A man with no mercy. Sex without respect. It hurt. She was never going to repeat that denial, she promised herself grimly as she began picking up plates from the table.

'Which bedroom did you choose? I need to go and make up the bed.'

There was a silence behind her; it trickled down her spinal cord like the scrape of a fingernail warning her that danger lurked behind.

It took the form of silk-like satire. 'Our son assures me that all his friends' parents sleep in the same bed.'

She spun back to find him leaning casually against the sink with his hands resting in his pockets. He was enjoying this, she realised. 'You're joking!' she insisted.

A single eyebrow mocked her horrified look. 'I was very impressed with his forward thinking,' Rafiq answered lightly. 'He gave me a choice. His room or your room. And since his room has only one small single bed in it and yours has a very large divan, I took the advice I was being offered and agreed to share—as parents do.'

'Well, I *don't* share!' She itched to swipe that mocking smile from his face. '*Never.* Do you understand?'

'Not even when we are man and wife?'

'I've changed my mind; I don't want to marry you!' she said. 'We—we will have to come to some other arrangement about sharing Robbie.'

'Now, that is one area in which *I* don't share,' he warned.

'And I won't marry a man who feels as bitter about me as I feel about him!'

'Then we are both on a learning curve.'

'Don't talk business-speak to me!' she snapped out angrily.

He leapt on her like a cat, picked her up and sat her down on the kitchen table, braced his hands beside her legs then pushed his dark face up close. 'Would you rather I woo you into accepting me?' he purred.

She stiffened like a cardboard cut-out; if he'd said it to insult her then he had certainly achieved his aim. 'I've been wooed by you before and I would rather have a snake do it.'

'Remove that ring one more time and you will regret it,' he warned very, very succinctly.

Melanie looked down and was surprised to find her fingers trying to work the ring loose. The threatened tears came back. 'I don't want you here,' she choked.

He saw the tears, touched a finger to the corner of her eye to capture one. 'Too late,' he announced, then stepped back.

He had heard what she had been too busy to hear—their son coming towards the kitchen. She leapt from the table just as Robbie appeared to take Rafiq off to watch his video. Melanie forced herself to tidy the kitchen, then went upstairs to make up the bed in the spare bedroom. It was a cold, dark little room with a cold little bed, and she had to grit her teeth as she made it so she would not let her conscience accept that a man of Rafiq's size would never be able to sleep in it—or at least he'd freeze trying, she added as she snubbed her nose at the room and walked out.

Robbie kept the atmosphere buoyant right up until she eventually coaxed him into bed. He fell asleep blissful in the knowledge that when he awoke his daddy would still be there.

By the time Melanie trudged back down the stairs she had developed a throbbing headache and was intending to go straight to the kitchen to find some painkillers when

she caught sight of Rafiq through the half-open door that
led into the living room. He was standing by the fire with
a hand thrust into his trouser pocket while the other held
a mobile phone to his ear. He was speaking in fluent
French. For a few seconds he even looked French, a
smooth, sleek and dauntingly sophisticated Frenchman
with the language for lovers falling from his lips.

It was not the cleverest of thoughts to have, she realised
as her senses rose to the invitation to remember the lover
once again. She made herself move on to the kitchen before he caught sight of her standing there looking at him
like some sex-obsessed idiot. It had been that kind of day!
A day packed full of old obsessions and new raging impulses. Sexual impulses; angry impulses. Her impulse to
go and seek him out; his impulse to lay siege and seduce.
The shocks, the grip of an old obsessive desire, the excitement in knowing they were both running out of control.

The headache got worse. She took two painkillers and
set about preparing a pot of coffee. He was standing in
more or less the same place when she carried the coffee
tray into the room. He was still on the telephone, speaking
in Spanish now, a language she recognised easily because
Sophia was half-Spanish and could tumble into the language when she was angry enough to need its extra fire.

He turned his dark head as he heard the tray rattle. Their
gazes clashed, and Melanie broke hers away. Five seconds
later the mobile was back in his pocket.

'Coffee?' she offered politely.

'Thank you, yes,' he replied. 'Black, no sugar.'

Black with no sugar, she repeated. Like the man himself:
dark and unsweetened. She poured the coffee, then handed
him his cup. He accepted it with a murmured, 'Thank you.'

She looked pale and tired, Rafiq noticed, and had to
smother the urge to sigh as he turned to look at the fire,
taking with him the image of Melanie sitting there on
faded velvet looking down at her coffee mug curled inside
fingers that looked bloodless and cold. Hell, he thought in

frustration, to him this whole house was cold. Even with the fire burning in the grate, the ancient central heating system only managed to take the edge of a subfreezing temperature! Despite his millions, and the loving attention he had poured into Rafiq's son, William Portreath had not poured much love into his home. It was virtually falling down around them. Everything in it came from a bygone century.

'Your requirements do not make any provision for the renovations this house clearly requires.'

Eyes like dark amber blinked at him. 'What are you talking about?'

'The papers you left with me,' he explained. 'They talk a lot about investments and trust funds but nothing about your annual expenditure or how much it is going to cost to bring this house into the twenty-first century.'

'I don't want to bring it into the twenty-first century. I like the house just as it is.'

She did? Was she lying just to go against him? 'It is cold in here, Melanie,' he said, stating the obvious. 'The walls are so cold that the wallpaper is peeling.' Not that its demise was much of a loss, he added with silent disdain. 'I, for one, see no reason why we should live like this.'

She bristled. 'Nobody is asking you to!'

He ignored that. 'I will employ someone to draw up some plans for renovation,' he announced.

Tired golden eyes began to sparkle. The mug was replaced on the tray. 'William has been gone only two months and you come in here wanting to obliterate thirty years of his life?' She rose stiffly. 'You will touch nothing,' she told him. 'It isn't yours to touch. And if you don't find that acceptable then you know what you can do!'

She was hurt; he could see it. Rafiq wanted to kick himself. Ridding himself of his cup, he offered her a deep bow. 'I have offended you,' he acknowledged. 'I apologise. It was not my intention to—'

'Y-you think I can't compare this—*home* to that super-expensive luxuriously blank space you like to live in?' she said, interrupting his apology. 'That I haven't noticed the way you've been looking on everything here with disdain? Does it offend your ego to know that your son loves this house?'

'No.' He denied that. 'I just think that it needs—'

'Well, forget it,' she said, cutting right across him a second time, and turned her stiff back towards him and walked to the door. 'You can use the room at the end of the landing. Be sure to make the fire safe before you go up. Now, goodnight.'

She'd left the room before he could speak another syllable, leaving him standing there feeling as if he'd just struck a woman for the first time in his life.

'Damn,' he muttered, and took the first step to go after her. Then on a heavy sigh changed his mind. She'd had enough for one day. He had had enough! 'Damn,' he cursed again, and turned back to the fire. It was dying fast, like the whole blasted day.

A car drew up outside the house. He listened to the sound of its door slamming shut. Another sigh and he was striding for the front door before Kadir could ring the doorbell and awaken Robert. I learn very quickly, he mused grimly as he reached out to take the suitcase from his aide.

'Thank you,' he grunted. 'I do not need to tell you that this situation is no one else's business.'

'No, sir. Of course, sir.'

He nodded, said goodnight and closed the door.

Upstairs Melanie listened to the car from the comfort of her duvet. She'd curled up beneath it after taking a shower in her *en-suite*, very ancient bathroom. Her teeth still chattered from the chills she'd given herself drying her body. She'd pulled on a knitted-cotton nightdress and was now only waiting for the duvet to infuse some warmth into her body.

Okay, she reasoned, so she knew the house needed a complete face-lift. She'd been wanting to do it for years, but William hadn't liked change. He'd been an old man who'd had a right to feel like that. And he did not deserve that some complete stranger should walk in here and start tearing his life down!

How dared he? Her throat caught on a muffled sob. How dared Rafiq believe he could just take over everything— even her bed if she let him get away with it!

The front door closed; she felt it reverberate through the floor beneath her bed. She'd heard Rafiq telling Robbie that someone was going to bring his suitcase here. Well, she hoped he'd changed his mind and had left with the delivery person! And on that final, wholly satisfying thought she closed her eyes and willed her icy feet to get warm so that she could just go to sleep. She had almost— almost—achieved both impossible feats when a curse in the darkness brought her swimmingly awake.

Suddenly the duvet was being lifted, to let the cold night air come into her warm cocoon. A short second later a body followed—a very cold, very naked body with an arm that clamped her to him and powerful limbs that curled snugly into hers.

'Oh, my God,' she gasped on a shocked little shiver. 'What do you think you are doing?'

'Getting warm,' Rafiq informed her grimly. Furious, she wriggled to get free. 'Stay still,' he gritted, close to her ear lobe.

He had to be joking! 'You could have had the decency to put some clothes on!'

'If my nakedness offends you then consider it punishment for that bed you prepared for me.'

He'd actually tried it? In a mulish kind of way Melanie was rather pleased that he had at least attempted to do the honourable thing. 'I don't want you here,' she protested nonetheless.

'The choice does not belong to you. Our son expects me to be in this bed when he wakes in the morning, and the other bed was an insult.' A hand on her shoulder turned her to face him; dark eyes glittered down into hers. 'You are a ruthless woman, Melanie Portreath,' he told her. 'Now it is my turn to be ruthless.'

And he was, in the way he wrapped himself around her, punishing her by stealing all her warmth, then punishing her again by falling fast asleep.

CHAPTER EIGHT

IT WAS a horrible weekend. There was not one single part of it that Melanie would have wanted to live through again. Daylight became an agony of hours watching her son sink himself into total hero-worship, and the nights an agony of too much intimacy with a man who clearly did not want more than to share her bed.

In his new role of father Rafiq dedicated himself to learning everything he could about his son. They talked, and they commandeered William's study, where Robbie hit Rafiq with a million questions, all of which his father answered with a considered seriousness that made Melanie's heart ache. Rafiq could do no wrong. She tried not to resent the way Robbie was turning to his father for everything. She tried to tell herself that this was what she had wanted, what she had hoped and aimed for when she had brought Rafiq into Robbie's life.

But it hurt to witness their growing closeness while she was required to contribute very little other than the odd smile or nod, or food when necessary. By the end of each day she was so exhausted playing the smiling little woman in the background that the moment Robbie was safely in bed she took herself off to bed too, leaving Rafiq to do what men like him did—use his evenings to work from the laptop computer that had arrived with his suitcase— before he came to slide into her bed, draw her in, sigh, then fall asleep.

She didn't understand him—didn't think she wanted to understand a man who could ravish her with a blind compulsion one minute then spend whole nights lying beside her and not offer one measly pass!

Their son loved the whole family scenario. In fact it made Robbie's day to run into their bedroom each morning and find both his parents wrapped snugly around each other. He couldn't be happier if he tried.

But for Melanie resentment sizzled across her senses; frustration throbbed in her loins. Had she sunk so low that she could become hooked on passion after a couple of quick sips?

Monday morning could not come quickly enough. She waved Rafiq off to work in his sharp dark business suit, and only did that because her son's hand was firmly attached to his father's. Rafiq was delivering Robbie to school, along with other children, as part of the morning school run!

I've been made redundant, she thought peevishly as she closed the front door. Daddy is the new rising star in the street and I am the fading one.

The jaded one, she corrected as her shoulders sagged wearily through lack of sleep and a whole truckload of tension. Standing there in the sudden quietness of the hallway, she actually took a moment to consider going upstairs and just crawling back beneath the duvet to sleep the rest of the day away while there was no Rafiq to spoil it for her.

But his presence was there in the bedroom, she remembered. His clothes hung with her clothes in the wardrobe; the scent of his soap permeated the adjoining bathroom.

You wanted this, she tried telling herself. You instigated the whole darn thing and, if anything, you should be pleased by how successful Robbie's introduction to his father has turned out, not standing here wilting like a wet leaf.

The light tap on the back door was a welcome diversion. Straightening her shoulders she walked into the kitchen just in time to watch Sophia step into the house.

'Hi,' Sophia murmured, and her expression could not have looked more sombre if she'd tried. In her hand she

held a newspaper, which she set down on the kitchen table.
'Take a deep breath, Melanie,' she suggested, 'because you
are not going to like this...'

Rafiq was sitting in his chair behind his desk in his beautifully warm centrally heated office wishing he dared close
his eyes and fall asleep because for these last miserable
nights he'd lain awake in that bed with Melanie and had
ached.

Ached. There was no better word for it. Was he a fool?
Was he going insane, playing it this coolly? Yes, he was
a fool, he accepted, because all it would have taken would
have been one touch and she would have been his for the
taking.

But he was out to prove a point. Melanie had hit him
hard with some of the things she had thrown at him. She
had made him out to be selfish and fickle. She had implied
he did not have it in him to stay the course. She believed
he would get weary of being a father and walk away when
the novelty wore off him.

She'd also told him he thought her cheap by tumbling
her into bed with him at the first opportunity. Which he
had done; he freely admitted it. But not for one moment
had he considered her cheap! Indeed, it had cost him a
very great deal because he had been so bowled over by
the strength of their feelings that he wanted to do it all
again and again—and again.

She had claimed he had made love to her eight years
ago then had despised her afterwards. Now she was waiting for him to despise her again. So sex was out of the
question until he had placed a wedding ring on her finger.
If that did not show her he meant serious business, then
nothing would.

So, he thought with grim impatience. He had arranged
a civil wedding service. From that day on he meant to have
everything: a wife, his son, and some serious passion—

preferably in a bedroom that did not send him into a par-
oxysm of shivers every time he stripped off his clothes.

And he had just the right place for this serious seduction.
He knew the day on which it was going to happen. Now
all he had to do was ring home and speak to half-brother,
Hassan.

'Where have you been hiding?' his brother demanded,
the moment the connection was made. 'I have been trying
to contact you all weekend.'

'It cannot have been urgent or Kadir would have found
me.'

'What intrigues me is why he refused to divulge to me
where you were.'

'I was busy,' he said, and could almost see Hassan's
grimace at his don't-go-there-tone. 'How is Father?'

He asked the usual question and he received back the
reassuring answer he was looking for. 'He is well and content.'

'And Leona?'

'The same—what is this, Rafiq?' Hassan put in curiously. 'You sound—different.'

Different? He grimaced. Different did not come close to
describing the changes in his life. 'Do you think it would
be safe to leave them for a couple of days?'

'Yes, if I have to.' But Hassan sounded puzzled. 'Is
there something wrong at the bank?'

'No, this is a—personal matter,' Rafiq answered coolly.
'I need you to do me a great favour. If you could be in
London on Friday I would much appreciate it.'

'Rafiq needs a favour?' Leona repeated as she lay on the
bed, letting her husband smooth oil into her swollen abdomen. 'Well, that has to be a first.'

'Not quite,' Hassan murmured. 'But it is certainly unusual for him to ask anyone for anything.'

Leona was frowning thoughtfully. 'Do you think this

business with Serena Cordero has upset him more than we thought it would?'

'Could be.' Hassan paused in his ministrations to kiss her frown away, then went back to his duties, long fingers smoothing oil over creamy white skin stretched taut across the mound that was their growing child. 'He has been acting strangely since the announcement of her marriage.' It was his turn to frown. 'I am reliably informed that he has hardly been to the bank since the newspaper article appeared and is almost impossible to track down. Nadia gets shifty if I ask questions, and so does Kadir. So I will have to go to London if only to quench my curiosity as to what it is he's up to.'

'Of course,' Leona agreed. 'But I hope you're just a bit worried about him, too.'

'Of course,' he mimicked. 'Do you want to roll over so I can rub this into your back now?'

'No, thank you.' She declined the offer. 'I am perfectly happy with what you are doing right now.'

'Witch.' He laughed, and came to lean over her, eyes like brown velvet gently mocking hers of saucy green. Late afternoon sunlight was pouring in through the grilled window, turning everything in the bedroom a burnished gold. Leona's hair shone like fire on the pillow; her porcelain skin wore a lustrous glow. She was exquisite in every way possible. 'Why did no one warn me that pregnant women were such rampant sex machines?' he murmured throatily.

'It is nature's secret weapon, aimed to keep husbands from straying to more slender delights.' She smiled.

A black eyebrow arched. 'Was that a deliberate dig at my father?'

'Like father, like son,' Leona quoted.

'Yes.' His frown returned. 'You don't think Rafiq could be planning revenge on Serena, do you?'

'I don't get the link.'

'There isn't one.' Lowering his eyes, he began gently stroking a point on her stomach where he could feel his child's heart beating steadily. Leona reached out and gently touched a fingertip to the point where his brows met across the bridge of his arrogant nose.

He glanced up, smiled, then sighed and lay back against the pillows. 'Rafiq was hit hard by a woman once before—about eight years ago,' he confided. 'She was a beautiful blonde creature with golden eyes and a mouth designed to turn a saint into a sinner. I must add that Rafiq has never been a saint. But he fell head over heels in love with this woman, then found out she was taking him for a fool.'

'Name?' Leona asked curiously.

'I cannot remember. She was as English as you are, though, and young—quite shockingly young for one filled with such calculation. She was a farmer's daughter, as I recall, and saw Rafiq as her ticket out of drudgery. He asked her to marry him then discovered she was sleeping with her step-cousin. Rafiq severed the relationship and that should have been the end of it.'

'But it wasn't?'

'No.' Hassan shook his head. 'She tried to contact him again many months later. It was the only other time that I can recall him asking me to do him a favour. She rang the London bank while I was there and Rafiq was here in Rahman, playing the nomad while still licking his wounds. She wanted to see him. When I relayed the message he asked me to meet with her to see if she was okay.'

'He still cared?'

'He was besotted.' His brother sighed out heavily. 'I have never seen him like that with a woman before or since.'

'So what did you do?'

'I had her checked out before I did anything. Discovered she was living with a man old enough to be her grandfather and, more to the point, was as heavily pregnant as you are now, my sweet.' He caught hold of her hand and kissed it. 'I arranged a meeting; she arrived expecting to see Rafiq. She tried convincing me that Rafiq was the father of her baby. So I told her what I thought Rafiq would do if she managed to convince him that this was true. She did not pursue the claim,' he concluded with grim satisfaction. 'A very nasty paternity battle through the courts was too much for her to take, apparently. She slunk off into the ether and was never heard from again.'

'But what if the child had been Rafiq's?'

'It was not,' he stated with absolute certainty. 'You know his background. If there had been the slightest possibility that he had made the woman pregnant he would have followed the prospect until he could be certain either way.'

'What did he say when you told him she was pregnant?'

'I didn't tell him,' he replied. 'I said I couldn't find her but that I'd heard she was living with some man. He never mentioned her name again.'

'Sometimes I really don't like you,' Leona informed him. 'You have a ruthless streak so wide it makes me shiver.'

'She was a woman on the make, Leona,' he said deridingly. 'People in our position meet them all the time. They see dollar signs up above our heads and latch on like limpets.'

'But still....'

'Rafiq caught her red-handed with her other lover.'

End of story. 'What a manipulating bitch,' Leona murmured, taking it personally that some woman would dare to use her beloved bother-in-law in such a way.

Rafiq had only just put the phone down when Kadir knocked at his door, then quietly let himself into the room. He was wearing the look of a man who was walking towards the gallows. Rafiq straightened in readiness, but nothing prepared him for what he was about to be hit with.

'My apologies, sir, but I think you should see this...' Carefully Kadir placed a newspaper onto the desk in front of Rafiq. With his usual efficiency his aide had folded the

English tabloid so that Rafiq needed only to glance down and see what it was Kadir was showing him.

There was Serena, smiling up at Carlos Montez. It was the same damn article, now reproduced in spiced-up English. Rafiq couldn't believe it. He shot to his feet. 'What the hell?' he muttered.

'Apparently Miss Cordero arrived in London this weekend, sir,' Kadir quietly explained. 'Her show opens at a West End theatre on Wednesday. The—er—article is by way of a promotion for this event. I thought...'

He was talking to fresh air because Rafiq was already striding across the room with the rolled-up newspaper clenched in his hand.

'H-How did you get hold of this?' Melanie asked Sophia.

'My grandmother likes to send me the Spanish newspapers to make sure I keep in touch with my roots,' Sophia explained.

Melanie nodded unhappily. 'And it says?' she prompted.

'You don't really want me to read it out to you again, Melanie,' Sophia murmured gravely. 'The point is that this paper is dated last Tuesday—which is the same day you went to see Rafiq...'

'Meaning what?' Her lips felt too cold and numb to move properly; her whole face felt very much the same.

'Meaning the guy was publicly dumped on the day you walked into his office. He was already out for someone's blood before he even saw you. Therefore I think you have to ask yourself the question whether his actions since have been motivated by this.'

'Saving face?'

'Yes.' Sophia sighed. 'To suddenly pull a wife and son out of the hat will turn the tables on Miss Cordero. It will appear as if she is the one who married on the rebound while he walked away from their relationship of over a year unscathed.'

Over a year... Melanie lowered her gaze to the two photographs printed side by side on the page. One was of the beautiful Serena Cordero standing with her handsome new husband. The other was of Rafiq standing with Serena. Her heart crashed against her ribcage, turning her insides to jelly, because the photograph was just as Robbie had described it: Rafiq wearing Arab clothes while the lady wore a red frilly dress. William had shown this photograph to her son but hadn't shown it to her. Everyone but her— including her son—seemed to know about Rafiq's beautiful long-standing Spanish mistress!

Did Rafiq love this woman? Was the luscious dark beauty what he really wanted, and now that he couldn't have her was he prepared to take anyone?

No, not just anyone, she grimly amended, but a woman who happened to come packaged with his son.

She thought about the phone call he had taken in his office when he hadn't spoken a single word. She thought about the look in his eyes as he'd listened to whoever had been on the other end of that phone, followed by the kiss before he'd coldly thrown her out.

Then she thought about the way he had found out about Robbie and had been forced to rethink his stance. Days later had come his sudden explosion of hot passion followed by nothing since.

Nothing.

She swallowed down a lump of nausea. Clearly he had tried to burn Miss Cordero out of his system and failed. She had been nothing but a substitute, and a disappointing one at that. I must have been, she thought painfully—because look at her! Black hair, black eyes and a lush-red passionate mouth looked back at her. Miss Cordero possessed the kind of sumptuous hourglass figure that most women would kill to own.

Which makes me the consolation prize.

She caught the sound of a key in the front door then. Only one person beside herself had a key to this house. Her insides became a mess of misery as she listened to

Rafiq call out her name. Sophia straightened in her chair, her eyes growing wide and dark and curious. Footsteps sounded on the polished wood floor as he strode towards the kitchen, then arrived to fill its doorway. Melanie tried focusing on his face, but all she saw was the shadowy outline of his whole dark bulk. Weakness feathered its way through the misery, because he did not fill the doorway with just his size, but with—everything. The darkness of his hair, his skin and his clothes said so much about him, and the stillness of every perfectly formed feature warned of the inner strength that so matched the outer shell.

His gaze flicked from her face to Sophia's face, then remained there. Melanie glanced at Sophia too, and was suddenly struck very hard by her friend's likeness to Serena Cordero. Another wave of nausea lodged in her throat, because he couldn't seem to take his eyes off her.

Rafiq had not expected to find Melanie with a visitor. For a moment he was struck numb by the thought that it was Serena herself, come to cause yet more trouble. Then the likeness faded and he glanced back at Melanie to find that she was looking down at the table. He saw the newspaper, felt his fingers clench around his own, and knew what Melanie was going to say before she even spoke.

'You have a mistress.'

'I *had* a mistress,' he corrected, coming further into the room as Sophia rose from her seat.

'I think I'll leave you both to it,' she murmured, and went to pick up the newspaper.

It was a gesture that did not pass by Rafiq. 'If the newspaper is yours, then I must assume you enjoy playing devil's advocate,' he drawled icily.

Sophia being Sophia, she took up the challenge in his tone. 'I don't like whatever it is you are trying to do here,' she informed him coolly.

Sparks began to fly. 'You believe I care one way or another what you like or dislike?'

The dark beauty's chin lifted, sending ripples of raven

hair flying over her shoulders. 'I don't think you care about anyone's feelings so long as you get your own way.'

'Well, I did not get my own way here,' he said, stabbing a long finger at the damning newspaper article.

It was then that he realised what it was he was stabbing at, and began to frown in confusion. While he was doing that Melanie got up and on a soft choke, rushed from the room. The urge to stop her was halted by his curiosity about this other woman.

His eyes narrowed. 'How did you get hold of this?' he demanded.

She shrugged. 'I am Spanish on my mother's side,' she explained. 'My grandmother sends me her newspapers once a week.'

'Industrious lady.'

'Very.'

'You have a point in hurting Melanie with this?'

'You are the one playing hurtful games with her feelings,' Sophia responded. 'I didn't like it from the beginning.' She let her glance fall to the newspaper. 'This tells me why I don't like it.'

And I do not like you, Rafiq thought as he looked into her face and saw a different face once again. She was so like Serena it could be the dancer standing there.

'You are on a face-saving exercise,' she dared to accuse him.

'What is your name?' he demanded.

'Sophia Elliot,' she announced, making his gaze narrow even further, because he had heard that name before. 'I am the next-door-neighbour from hell, Mr Al-Qadim,' she informed him, with a cool humour that confirmed the impression he had gained from his son that this woman was as tough as she was beautiful. 'I am also a pretty good lawyer,' she added. 'So if you are thinking of trying to bully Melanie into accepting a situation she doesn't really want, then try thinking again,' she advised. 'Because it is my belief you don't give a fig for her feelings, and Melanie

and Robbie have taken enough over this last year without
you using them as a method of deflecting your little embarrassment with the—'

'Name of the law firm you work for?' he cut in coolly.
She told him.

With a curt nod he stepped up to open the back door.
'You come and go via this route, I believe?'

'How did you know that?'

Because his son had been as admiringly vocal about his
aunt Sophia as he was about William Portreath. 'Trouble
rarely enters by conventional means, Miss Elliot,' he replied, knowing that she would work out his source later.
But for now she was simply too busy bristling.

'I don't think you have the right to—'

'May I suggest that you mention my name to your em-
ployer before you begin informing me of my rights?' Rafiq
drawled coolly.

'Is that a threat?' she demanded.

Rafiq's answer was a polite bow of his head meant to
leave the question open to interpretation. 'Good day to
you, Miss Elliot,' was all he said.

But the woman had sense, Rafiq allowed, as he watched
her self-confidence begin to waver. She wasn't sure about
him and therefore took the wiser route: lifting her chin and
stepping through the door.

He closed it behind her, took a moment to grit his teeth.
Then he was moving across the kitchen on his way to find
Melanie. He located her in the bedroom, where she stood
in the window gazing out on yet another cold grey frost-
grained day. The room was no warmer, the woman in it
was as cold as ice. Anger roared. A bloody anger aimed
at Serena, at the press, Miss Elliot and anyone else who
thought they could meddle in his life!

'Your cynical friend stole my thunder,' he announced
very grimly.

'Don't try telling me you came back here to confess
your sins.'

'It is not a sin for a single man to maintain a mistress,' he countered. 'And I was referring to…this.'

'This' arrived on the tallboy beside her left shoulder. Melanie turned to see what it was he was talking about. It might have been Sophia's Spanish newspaper, only the glaring headline shouted at her in English and the date printed on it was today's. It was one of the more down-market British tabloids.

'Now you may read the whole article for yourself,' Rafiq said cynically. 'It has been spiced up since the original Spanish version was written. But—please…' he flicked a long hand in invitation '…enjoy—if you are into this kind of trash.'

'I never read newspapers.'

He had noticed their lack of evidence about the house. 'Well, read this one,' he advised, shot back a shirt-cuff, then strode towards the door.

'Where are you going?'

'I have things to do.'

'Aren't you even going to explain about this?'

'What is there to explain?' he countered. 'Serena Cordero and I were lovers until recently. But that, and the fact that she decided to use this very public source to announce the end of that relationship, has nothing to do with you, quite frankly.'

'It does when that announcement also came on the same day that I went to see you.'

'You see this coincidence as significant?'

She folded her arms across her body again. 'You changed,' she told him. 'After you took a call on your mobile. It was her on the phone, wasn't it? That call gave you the idea of using me to save your face.'

'It crossed my mind,' he admitted. 'But if you recall, Melanie, I still threw you out.' She flinched at the reminder. He nodded in acceptance of what that flinch represented. 'And if you believe that anything I have done since then has been due to a need to *save my face*, then there is really nothing left for me to say here.' With that he turned back to the door.

'Then why did you bother to come back here now?'

'Courtesy,' he said icily. 'I believed I owed you the courtesy of an explanation for why this article appeared in the newspaper today. But since you and your—friend have already dissected the week-old version, I see I wasted my time.'

'Wasted nearly a whole week of your time,' she murmured bitterly.

He paused. 'What is that supposed to imply?'

'I am not going to marry you.'

'Why not?'

She lowered her eyes. 'You're in love with her. She's what you really want.'

He laughed; it was harsh. 'If I'd wanted to marry Serena I could have done so at any time over the last year,' he announced. 'But what interests me here is that you seem to be thinking that loving someone is a prerequisite for marriage.'

'I don't think that.' She stiffened. 'I just don't want to marry a man who is pining for someone else.'

'Pining?' he repeated.

'It's obvious.' She shrugged, then made the big mistake of glancing at the bed.

His dark gaze followed suit. One of those awful tense silences they were so good at developing began to sing in the room. Hot colour flooded her complexion; she spun back to the window, wishing the man wasn't so good at reading her like an open book!

Did she have to be so obvious? she railed at herself. Did it always—always—have to be this man who made her feel like a lovesick fool?

Sex-sick, she then corrected. God, she hated herself sometimes. 'Go, if you're going,' she snapped. Make it quick and don't come back!

'I have changed my mind.'

'Not on my account.' She tried to recover lost ground.

But she should have known by now that this man gave nothing back once he had gained it. She heard a rustle, felt a shot of alarm shoot down her backbone, spun, then just stood there staring in open dismay as the jacket to his suit hit the floor.

'Come any closer and I'll start screaming,' she warned, backing herself into the window as he began walking towards her with fingers smoothly loosening his tie.

'Scream,' he invited. 'Who will come? Your cynical friend from next door?' Reaching over her shoulder, he tugged the cord that closed the heavy curtains. The room was suddenly shrouded in darkness. A dangerous glitter burned in his eyes. 'Think of the embarrassment, Melanie, if Miss Elliot was foolish enough to come running in here only to find you begging in my arms.'

'I will never beg!' She gave an angry push at his body.

He laughed, low and deep and tauntingly. 'One kiss and you will not be able to stop yourself,' he derided. 'Do you think I have not been aware that you have hardly slept a wink in that bed because you want me so badly?'

'That's a lie.'

He kissed her. It was no lie. She dived, she fell, she almost—almost begged him. Her breathing went haywire, her senses caught alight, and she whimpered into his urgent mouth. His arms imprisoned her, but they didn't need to. She was clinging tightly.

'I hate you for doing this.'

'But, as you see, I am not pining for a lost love,' he murmured, and to punctuate his meaning he caught hold of one of her hands and placed it down his front, then caught her protesting little gasp in his mouth.

Desire pulsed with every hammering heartbeat; it bounced off the walls and back at her in wave after wave of blistering passion, battering her every sense into submission. They kissed; they lost their clothes with an urgent lack of finesse. Somehow they managed to make it to the bed; his hand grabbed the duvet and stripped it back from the mattress before he tumbled her down on it. They kissed some more; they rolled; he stretched her out and ravished her breasts, then placed a line of hot wet kisses down her front; he buried his mouth between her thighs. She almost leapt into the air in shock, then went wild, utterly wanton. Bright hot lights were propelling themselves at her eyelids; she couldn't keep still and his hands had to clamp her hips so he could sustain the torment until she lost herself completely, lost him, lost everything.

When she opened heavy eyelids she found black eyes glittering down at her, his face a smouldering cast of raw sensuality made all the more potent by triumph. 'You shouldn't have done that,' she whispered.

'Why not?' The hand he used to push the damp hair away from her face was trembling.

'Because...' she breathed. He hadn't leapt with her, and she wanted him to leap with her. It was essential that he lose touch with himself as she had, or what had he proved here except that he was the expert and she was just somebody, nobody—anybody?

So she pushed him onto his back and came to lean over him, calling upon instincts she had never used before to take him where she had just been. He lay in the darkness and let her do whatever she wanted. She kissed his shoulders, his chest, sucked deeply on the hard points of his male nipples, stroked her hands down his body when he groaned hoarsely, took her mouth on a journey that stopped at nothing. His fingers coiled into her hair and his laboured breathing drove her on. When he shifted to grasp her beneath her arms then drag her upwards for a kiss that devoured she was ready for him to finish what she had started with the deep, urgent thrust of his pelvis.

They shuddered together into a drumming ecstasy; he seduced her mouth until the very last whisper of pleasure had faded, and eventually she lay heavily upon him, limp and useless. She couldn't even draw enough energy to care that once again she had given him more of herself than she had ever wanted to.

She belonged here. It was that simple—and that sad.

'We marry as soon as possible,' he announced suddenly. Then, before she could raise so much as a gasp in protest, he switched their position and began the whole wild adventure all over again.

CHAPTER NINE

MELANIE sat in a chair beside Sophia and carefully rotated her aching shoulders. 'Can't I just wear that one?' she said hopefully.

'If you want to look like a fairy on a Christmas tree, of course you can wear that dress,' Sophia replied.

'Don't be cruel.'

'Do you want to knock his eyes out?'

'No—yes.' Melanie sighed and fiddled with a drink-starved wilting rosebud. 'I wish he wasn't so determined to make all of this fuss about a silly civil wedding.'

'I still can't understand why you are going through with it,' Sophia said with a disapproving snap.

'You've seen him with Robbie, Sophia,' Melanie reminded her. In an effort to get Sophia and Rafiq to stop sniping at her about each other she had invited Sophia round for drinks. Rafiq had been about to take Robbie to bed when she'd arrived. She had caught him holding his son in his arms, accepting the kind of love-shining hugs Melanie had witnessed many times. 'They adore each other. I couldn't stop this now even if I wanted to,' she concluded heavily.

'Do you want to?'

She hesitated a bit too long without answering.

'So you're the sacrificial lamb.' Sophia sighed.

Oh, yes, Melanie thought. I sacrifice myself every night in his arms.

Getting up, she walked back to the rail filled with frothy white dresses and began flicking restless fingers along the selection. Why did she let him get away with it? she was asking herself crossly. Had she no pride left at all?

She knew the trigger that set him off each time. It was called Serena Cordero. Plant the beautiful Spaniard's name into his head and he responded by diving into sex like a man in search of blind escape!

But you dive right in there with him, she admitted. In fact you only have to start thinking about diving in and you break out in a hot sweat.

'I'll try this one,' she said, choosing a gown at random which she passed to the hovering assistant who carried it off to the dressing room.

Sophia waited until the woman had gone out of earshot before she said tentatively, 'Melanie...have you thought about when you're married to him and things become... intimate?'

'Are you joking?' she gasped.

But, no, Sophia wasn't joking, she realised. She was actually looking like a rather anxious mother hen trying to prepare her innocent chick for what the big bad rooster did.

'I'm sorry to disillusion you about me, Sophia,' she responded. 'But what do you think we have been doing in my home all this time?'

For the first time ever she saw shock then embarrassment flood her tough friend's face. 'You mean you—'

The words dried up. Melanie laughed; it sounded strangled. She spun back to face the rail. The silence between them sizzled with the kind of images that just did not belong in this pretty shop adorned with chaste and virginal white.

'But I thought—'

'Well, don't think,' Melanie cut in on a tight little mutter. Her cheeks were hot. Sophia's cheeks were hot. What was it about people that they believed they could make assumptions about her? Rafiq believed she was a sex-hungry wanton; Sophia believed she was about as naive and dumb as a woman with a seven-year-old child could possibly be!

Maybe this was a good time for the assistant to reappear, because she helped to carry them over a very uncomfortable moment. Melanie scowled at the dresses on display and wondered what Rafiq would do if she turned up to their wedding in her best black suit?

A beautifully manicured hand appeared to one side of her. 'You are your own worst enemy, aren't you?' Sophia murmured sombrely. 'Here,' she said, 'try this…'

Sophia had pulled a misty-blue silk suit out from amongst the swathes of white. Her whole attitude altered from that moment on. She's given up on me, Melanie realised as she wriggled into the fitted blue suit. I've put myself beyond redemption.

But then I placed myself beyond that when I let him make love to me knowing he was using me to block out another woman, she acknowledged helplessly.

She bought the misty-blue suit. It looked right somehow—made her legs seem longer and her hair more golden, made her eyes glow a deeper shade.

'What do you think?'

Rafiq was standing in the hallway of Melanie's house while Ethan Hayes was still looking about him with an interested eye. 'You must already know that it has tremendous potential,' Ethan told him. 'But I don't know how you expect to modernise the whole house while still maintaining every worn-out feature.'

'There is an old man's life etched into those features,' Rafiq explained. 'Can we not give the shell an uplift, then simply put everything else back the way it is now?'

'I am an architect, not a miracle-worker,' Ethan said dryly 'The heating is useless, the fires belch smoke, the floorboards creak worryingly and the walls seem to be warning anyone that dares go near them not to remove a single picture unless you want them to fall down. All of that can be put right,' he stated. 'But the wallpaper will have to be hand-reproduced, the furniture will need to be sent away for some careful renovation, and nothing we replace will have the patina of age it wears now. I have a worrying suspicion that the deeper we look, we will find wet and dry rot, not to mention woodworm. You need Leona on this, not me, Rafiq,' he concluded.

'Leona is busy with other things,' Rafiq reminded him. 'I just wanted your opinion before I decided whether to go ahead.'

'It would be simpler to gut it and start from scratch,' Ethan advised. 'You only have to look at the other houses on this street to see what it can look like, given the chance.'

'I have no wish to make it look like the others.' This was his son's home, the place where Robert and Melanie had found love and security. Aesthetically it must not change. Structurally, he feared it had no choice.

'If Leona is out of action, then what if I hand the project over to my wife?' Ethan suddenly suggested.

'To your *wife*?' Rafiq couldn't hide his surprise.

Ethan turned a rueful grin on him. 'Yes, I do mean the flighty piece who spent the evening flirting with you a couple of months ago,' he confirmed lazily. 'She has hidden talents,' he confided. 'One of those talents being a very impressive track record in house renovation.'

Rafiq was momentarily diverted. In the space of just a few short weeks, earlier this year, Ethan Hayes had gone from being a serious enemy of the Al-Qadim family to being a good close friend due to falling into love with Eve, the provocative granddaughter of the Greek tycoon Theron Herakleides.

'The lovely Eve renovates old property for a living?' Rafiq could not withhold his disbelief.

'She shocked me with it too,' Ethan confessed. 'On the morning after we returned from our honeymoon, in fact, when she came to breakfast wearing overalls and put a builder's hat down on the table. She's been buying, renovating and selling on houses in London for years—as a hobby, apparently. Loves to get her fingernails chipped, has an affinity with dirt and grime. Give her a lump hammer and she will have that wall down in half an hour.'

His eyes were glowing with amusement. But beneath the amusement was a love and pride that made Rafiq want to sigh. At home in Rahman his brother was no doubt relaxing with the woman he adored with every breath that he took. And here stood Ethan Hayes so in love with his lovely, if highly provoking, wife, that he could not keep his feelings from showing on his face.

And here I stand, planning to marry a mere obsession, he mused heavily. A past obsession, a present obsession, but most importantly of all a sexual obsession. Upstairs their bedroom had become a place for hot and tumultuous orgies. Melanie had revealed a capacity to take eagerly whatever he chose to offer in that bed upstairs. But what really ravaged him was not knowing if she responded to any man in the same mind-blowing way.

He swung away so that Ethan Hayes could not see his expression. Sometimes he wished he had never come here, had never given in to the temptation that was Melanie Portreath. She turned him inside out, made him behave as he had never behaved in his life before. Which made him—what?

A man in love with his obsession? The words filtered like poison into his brain tissue, sending him on yet another restless swing that concluded with him frowning at his watch. Melanie was due back soon from the hours she donated to Robbie's school several mornings a week, helping out wherever she was required to do so. He did not want her to find him here with Ethan Hayes.

'Have you no ambition to do anything with your life?' he had asked her one evening.

'Should I be ashamed of wanting to be a full-time mother to my son?' she'd bristled indignantly by return.

'No, of course not. I just thought—'

'Well, don't think,' she'd snapped. 'I am comfortable

with who I am, but if you're not then you know what you can do.'

Leave. She never failed to let him know that the option was there for him to use if he wished to do so. He usually answered by kissing her breath away. But would she care if he did leave? Or would she heave a sigh of relief as she watched him walk away from this idea that marriage between them could work?

'I would like work to begin while the owners are away,' he said to Ethan with a calmness that belied what was going on inside his head. 'It will be less painful for those concerned if they do not have to witness the initial destruction of everything they love.'

'Who owns the house?' Ethan questioned.

'A—friend of mine.' He couldn't even say the words, My wife, as of the day after tomorrow, which angered him all the more. Was he ashamed? Was he afraid it might never happen? She was still having second thoughts despite the torrid sex; he was aware of that. Recently she had even withdrawn the sex. She had turned a cold shoulder upon him and said she had a headache.

A headache. The oldest excuse in a woman's vocabulary. He frowned, glanced at the time again but did not register it because he was remembering that she had spent yesterday out with her cynical friend, choosing something to wear for her wedding day. Ten minutes alone with Miss Elliot would have been long enough for Melanie to begin piling on the doubts.

'Then this house cannot be touched without her permission.' Ethan's voice intruded on his own dark thoughts.

The very walls seemed to move, as if William Portreath's ghost was stirring himself to warn Rafiq to be careful how much he took for granted. I take nothing for granted, he grimly told the old ghost.

'You said it is in danger of falling down,' he responded.

'Yes,' Ethan confirmed. 'But you will still need written permission from the owner to touch it, Rafiq,' he advised.

'Even my flighty wife would not dare come near it without written consent from the owner.'

'I will obtain it.' He nodded. By fair means or foul, he added silently, thinking of the trust with which Melanie signed any papers either he or Randal Soames placed in front of her.

Which was just another thing about Melanie that irritated him. The money she now possessed meant nothing. Her son and this house meant everything.

Where did he fit in?

The telephone in William's study began ringing. Since he had commandeered the room for himself, Rafiq assumed the call must be for him, and excused himself, leaving Ethan to wander the house some more while he went to lean against William's old desk and lifted the receiver to his ear.

'Yes?' he said brusquely.

There was a small silence, then a tentative-sounding voice. 'Is Melanie there?'

Rafiq froze on instant recognition of that deep country burr. 'No,' was all he could manage to utter.

'Oh…' Jamie Sangster sounded momentarily nonplussed. 'Who are you?' he then asked curiously.

'A—friend,' Rafiq gritted.

Another 'Oh' raked his eardrum, followed by, 'Will you give her a message for me, then? Tell her that Jamie will be in town on Saturday and could she give me a ring so we can arrange dinner or something to talk about her proposition?'

Rafiq replaced the receiver without replying. He then carefully removed it from its rest. Beyond the study door he could hear Ethan Hayes moving about the hallway. In William Portreath's study the only sound was the buzzing taking place inside his own head.

* * *

Melanie signed all the papers Rafiq set in front of her without bothering to look at them. She was so tired she knew she couldn't see straight to read them anyway.

'Randal tells me you have decided to set a separate fund aside,' Rafiq murmured levelly. 'Is it for anything special?'

'Is Randal supposed to pass on to you every decision I make?' She frowned.

'Taking care of your money is what you signed me up to do for you.'

Shame this relationship hadn't stayed that simple, Melanie thought heavily and got up from the desk with the grim intention of taking herself off to bed. She was exhausted beyond anything—stress and tension—tension and stress...

'So, what is the money set aside for?' Rafiq prompted an answer.

'Personal stuff,' she said.

'A million pounds of it?'

His sarcasm showed. Melanie turned to look at him. There was something different about him tonight. He'd been quiet and withdrawn, even with Robbie. And he looked paler than he usually did. Was the stress of it all getting to him also?

'I might want to go on a spending binge.' She attempted to make light of a tricky subject. 'Your know, retail therapy and all that.'

He didn't even try to smile. 'You believe you may require such therapy once married to me?'

She glanced at him, standing there in so-called casual clothes that had clearly cost the earth. 'Well, my one good suit doesn't look much next to the dozen or so suits you have hanging in my wardrobe,' she pointed out wryly.

'It will not cost a million to replenish your wardrobe.'

'I might decide I want to by loads of things—like a new car or two,' she suggested. 'Why, is there a ceiling on how much I am allowed to stash on one side?'

'No,' he answered quietly. 'But I think you have overdone it a little. Why not allow me to place, say—one hundred thousand in your account to be going on with?' he suggested. 'You need only say when you require more.'

Melanie shifted tensely; she did not want to talk about this. 'Don't talk down to me just because you know more about money than I do, Rafiq,' she told him crossly. 'If I'd wanted only one hundred thousand I would have made it only one hundred thousand.'

With that she went to leave the room.

'Where are you going?' His dark voice came after her.

'I'm tired. It's been a—long day. I want a nice soak in a warm bath, then just to fall asleep as soon as my head hits the pillow.'

'What—again?' he drawled lazily.

It was like a red rag to a bull. She whipped around to look at him. It was a terrible—terrible mistake. He was leaning against the edge of William's desk with his arms loosely folded and eyes slightly hooded by long black lashes, as usual.

Why? Because he was trying to impose another woman's image over her image. He wanted that other woman so badly that sometimes she could actually feel him ache.

'We aren't even married yet and you sound like a husband,' she lashed out. 'There has to be more to this relationship than just sex, or we are about to make a big mistake.'

The light from the desk lamp was playing across his bold dark features. She thought she saw a different kind of light glint in his eyes and stiffened her shoulders in readiness for him to throw something really nasty back at her like, Be grateful we have sex!

But he didn't say that. In fact he didn't saying or do anything but study her, and she felt herself begin to tremor, felt her inner self wanting to reach out for him with a desperation that made her want to cry. Simple eye contact and she was falling into that terrible pit. Her senses came alive, slinking terrible temptations down her quivering spine.

Then the heavy eyelids lowered even further. He began to straighten and her senses went haywire. If he starts walking, I start running, she told herself agitatedly. I don't want him to touch me—I don't! But what he did was unfold his arms and drop them to his sides before offering her one of those cold, curt formal bows he could demonstrate with such devastating effect.

'Of course,' he said. 'My apologies. Forgive my crass instincts,' he begged.

There was nothing crass about his instincts. Nothing crass about the way he could turn himself into this coldly polite, lofty giant of a stranger who contrarily made her want to be very gentle with him.

Her stomach muscles quivered; her heart began to ache. 'Rafiq...'

He turned away from the husky little murmur of his name, and picked up the papers she had just signed for him. 'I will be leaving early in the morning and will not be returning here tomorrow night. Robert knows this, but please reassure him that I will ring before his bedtime.'

All of a sudden she didn't know if she was standing on her head or her heels. Her emotions were flipping over from one thing to another; now she was experiencing stark fear.

'Y-you mean you're not coming back at all?' she managed to stammer.

He sent her a glance, a fleeting glance. 'A car will collect you on Friday morning. Please attempt not to be late.'

A car. Friday. Don't be late. She almost sank to her knees in relief. Which said it all really, didn't it? she accepted bleakly. I'm hooked. I can't bear the thought of living without him.

'Yes,' she whispered. 'Goodnight,' she said, and got herself out of there before her knees actually did give out.

Rafiq sat in the back of his chauffeur-driven car and stared out of the window at yet another cold, wet day in London.

Beside him his aide, Kadir Al-Kadir, sat quietly. He was in shock, but then who would not be to find himself hauled out of his bed at six in the morning by a man who was not happy that his plans were already beginning to fall apart?

Hassan had not made it to London. Something had come up involving important matters of state. If he had not been so stubborn and had told Hassan exactly why he wanted him here then his half-brother would have left no stone unturned in his quest to be at his side on this day. But that had not been the way he wanted to play it. Hassan had met Melanie eight years ago, during the weekend they'd spent on the Maitland estate. He knew the history of their relationship and had no kind thoughts for Melanie. Given enough time and the opportunity, he would have tried to stop the marriage today.

But he had still wanted his brother at his side on this important day for him, so he had planned Hassan's arrival to give him neither time nor space to voice his objections. As the old ones liked to say about meticulous planning, it simply begged to fall apart on you, he mused heavily.

He glanced at his watch. Thirty minutes to go. Melanie should be leaving home with their son and her cynical friend about now. 'Check what is happening with the other car,' he instructed Kadir.

The younger man located his mobile telephone. A few murmured questions later and he was putting it away again. 'The car is still awaiting its passengers, sir,' he informed him.

Rafiq nodded, slid a long finger across the tense line of his mouth and wished he hadn't asked the question. He would not do so again, he determined. Which meant he now had to endure a very tense half-hour.

'Ready?' Sophia asked.

No, Melanie thought. 'Yes,' she answered quietly.

'You look so pretty, Mummy,' Robbie told her. 'Doesn't she look pretty, Aunt Sophia?'

'Stunning,' Sophia agreed with a touch of dry cynicism. 'Now all she needs to do is smile to show she's happy about this.'

'Of course she's happy.' Robbie was jumping up and down with excitement. 'She's getting married to my daddy today.'

'Go and check if the car is still there, Robbie,' Sophia instructed. 'The innocence of youth.' She sighed as Robbie bounced out of the room and went clattering down the stairs. 'One good look at your face and he would know you are about to fall into a maidenly swoon.'

'Don't be so Gothic,' Melanie said. 'I'm fine. I just didn't sleep much last night.'

'Missed your man?'

Missed him dreadfully, she thought hollowly. Which only made the ache she was carrying around inside worse.

A telephone began ringing downstairs. 'I'll get it!' Robbie shouted.

'The big man is checking up on you,' Sophia wagered. 'He can't be certain that you are going to turn up.'

'Yes, he can. He only has to think about his son to know that I am going to be there— You look fantastic,' she put in when Sophia opened her mouth to say something Melanie knew she did not want to hear.

Her friend was wearing a dark purple suit that followed her hourglass figure to perfection. With her exotically dark colouring she made Melanie feel washed out and ordinary in her misty-blue outfit with its short straight skirt and nipped-in jacket edged with soft blue fake fur at the round neck and cuffs.

A rush of nerves suddenly washed through her, sending her heart down to her neat blue shoes. 'I don't think—'

Robbie came running down the landing 'Can we can go now—please?' he begged.

'You're not wearing something old,' Sophia murmured as they moved down the landing.

Melanie wriggled her diamond ring at her.

'Something borrowed?'

The hesitation was only slight before Melanie wriggled the self-same ring. Which said a lot as to how long she expected this marriage to last.

'Who was on the phone, Robbie?' she asked her son as they hit the downstairs hallway.

'Uncle Jamie,' he replied. 'I told him you were getting married to my daddy today and he rang off without saying goodbye.'

Melanie's footsteps stilled on the polished wood floor. But Robbie's moved him onwards to pull open the front door. Ice-cold air rushed into the house and she shivered. A man wearing a dark overcoat stood just outside, holding up a huge black umbrella. He saw Robbie and Sophia into the car and out of the pouring rain first. As Melanie stood there on the doorstep, waiting for him to return for her, she experienced the only real moment where she actually thought she was going to change her mind. Then the driver came back to offer her shelter; his smile was warm. She stepped out of the house, closing the door behind her.

Rafiq was standing with Kadir in the elegant foyer belonging to one of London's local government town halls when the entrance doors suddenly opened and his son, Melanie and her friend appeared. His son ran straight towards him. Miss Elliot became busy brushing away the few raindrops that had caught her clothes; Melanie looked at him and went perfectly still.

His heart began to pound against his ribcage; his legs suddenly felt heavy and weak. His son was talking away to him but he did not hear a single word. She was so lovely she tore at his senses, enchanting, shy and uncertain, like the younger woman he'd used to know.

'Stay here, Robert,' he instructed, and made himself

walk towards Melanie. As he came to a halt in front of her he saw her eyelashes flicker just before she looked up at him. 'So this is it,' he said with a smile that did not quite make it.

'Yes.' The single word whispered nervously from her. Her gaze drifted away. Her cheeks were pale and her fingers were trembling.

'I'm sorry we're a few minutes late,' she said in a little rush. 'The rain…'

The words became muffled by a smothering breathlessness as she picked up the aroma of his scent. He was wearing another midnight-blue suit made of a crease-free touch-temptingly smooth fabric. His shirt was so white it made his skin look darker and temptingly smooth like the suit. Her fingers twitched nervously against the little blue purse she was holding, and she kept her eyes averted in case she did something stupid like come jolting to her senses.

Was she really about to marry this tall dark beautiful man? 'W-where do we go?'

It was all she could think to say in the circumstances.

'Up the stairs.' He offered his hand to her. 'Shall we go?' he said.

There was another moment of complete stillness while Melanie stared at his hand. They never touched, unless compelled to do so by that awful sexual force. Did he know that? Was he aware that his outstretched hand was breaking new ground here? Her mouth ran dry; she tried to swallow. From the sidelines she caught sight of Sophia, watching them. Her friend too had noticed her hesitation and was probably making her own deductions as to what it meant.

The fact that Rafiq had noticed Sophia studying him showed when he turned his head to flash her a look. Sophia dared to cock a mocking eyebrow. Hostility sparked into life. Melanie responded by lifting up a hand and placing it in his. The gesture brought his gaze flashing back her

way, and his fingers closed gently round hers. Warm
strength enclosed icy frailty; something very dramatic began to build in the air. As he turned them towards the
elegant stairway that led to an upper foyer she noticed
Kadir Al-Kadir standing quietly to one side, with his dark
gaze fixed on Robbie as if he could not quite believe what
his eyes were telling him.

By necessity Rafiq made the polite introduction, though
Melanie suspected he did not want to speak at all. He was
tense; she was tense. They moved up the stairs together,
with Robbie dancing behind them, his hand tucked into
Sophia's, blissfully unaware of the stress-load weighing
down everyone else's shoulders.

Not twenty minutes later they were walking down those
same stairs again. It had all been so quick, so efficient—
so impersonal. But in those few minutes she had changed
her name to Al-Qadim and was now wearing a wedding
band on her finger. Even more disturbing was the ring
Rafiq had given her to slide on his long brown finger.

That hand now rested at the base of her spine, and remained there until they stepped outside. The rain was still
bouncing off the pavements. Three cars now stood in a
row at the kerb, with three black-coated men standing beside them holding black umbrellas over their heads.

With a click of his fingers Rafiq brought one man running. With a brief word of thanks he sent Kadir on his
way. Next came Melanie's first shock, when the second
man was brought running and she found herself being
hugged by Sophia, who murmured, 'Surprise, surprise. I
am taking your son off your hands until tomorrow.'

'But I don't want—'

'Not your choice any more, little sacrificial lamb,'
Sophia informed her dryly, only to be replaced by Robbie,
who was demanding a hug from his mother and excitedly
explaining all the things he and Sophia had planned for
the day, before he was ushered beneath the umbrella and
hurried away.

Standing there, shell-shocked beyond speech, Melanie found herself left alone with the man she had just married, watching another car move off, which left only one—a long, low-squatting animal thing with darkened glass and a distinct air of menace about it.

The snap of Rafiq's fingers set her blinking; the return of his hand to the base of her spine had her tensing jerkily. The last black-coated man came running with an umbrella. She was directed beneath it and into the warm soft depths of black-leather car seats. Rafiq followed, the car door closed with a smooth soft thud and they were alone— really alone—encased in dark glass and hidden, even from the driver.

Silence arrived. It hummed between them. The car began moving away from the kerb. She turned to look at Rafiq and found him looking back at her. His wide shoulders hugged the upholstered corner of the car and one ankle rested easily across the other knee with a set of long fingers lightly clasping the ankle. He looked relaxed, at ease, like a lazy cat contentedly at peace. Indeed, slumberous lashes barely flickered as he studied her face. But there was nothing relaxed about those devil-dark eyes hiding behind the lashes. They glinted in a way that sent tiny hot frissons chasing down her spine.

'I can't believe you planned all of this without my knowledge,' she said, jumping nervously into speech.

'It is tradition for a newly married couple to spend this time alone.'

'This isn't a traditional marriage.' That short ceremony they had just performed mocked the very word. 'We did this for Robbie, so why shouldn't he be here with us now?'

'Robbie is perfectly happy doing what he is doing.'

Well, I'm not, Melanie thought, and with a pressing together of her lips she turned her face away. Beyond the darkened glass she could see London moving past at speed. They were crossing one of the bridges that spanned the river, she realised, and she felt those frissons chase through her again, because they didn't need to cross the river to get to her house or even his apartment.

'Where are we going?' she asked sharply.

'To a place where my sacrificial lamb can perform in complete privacy,' he murmured silkily.

CHAPTER TEN

His reply tugged her face around to him again. He was smiling, but it wasn't a nice smile. Obviously he had overheard Sophia and, despite appearances to the contrary, he was actually as angry as hell.

'I am nobody's sacrifice,' she objected.

'Shame,' he drawled. 'I was looking forward to watching you lay yourself out on some softly sprung, silk-covered altar, then offer yourself to me.'

His description conjured up exactly the image it had aimed to. Heat stole into her cheeks; she bristled in annoyance with it. 'Back to sex again,' she derided.

'Would you prefer it if we discussed other things?'

'Like what?' she asked warily.

'Jamie,' he inserted with velvet precision. 'Our son tells me he spoke to his *uncle* Jamie on the telephone this morning, but he rang off before he could invite him to come to our wedding.'

At last she understood where the anger was coming from. 'I never said that—'

'Our son has a very generous nature,' he cut in. 'He seems to hold a great affection for his uncle Jamie. Do you think this affection has anything to do with how close he came to having Jamie as his father instead of me?'

Melanie released a sharp gasp. 'That is a terrible thing to say!'

'But the truth.'

'You don't *know* the truth!'

'He is still in your life. That is a clear truth.'

'I don't—'

'Do not begin this marriage by lying to me,' he gritted warningly.

Melanie took a deep breath to stop herself from exploding. 'I was about to say that I don't think that is any of your business,' she said coldly.

'From now on everything that you do is my business.'

'Does that mean everything that you do is my business too?' she tossed back. 'In this country we believe in equality. So why don't you tell me all about Serena Cordero.'

'You are trying to divert me from the main issue here.'

'That is because I have nothing to say on the subject,' she declared stubbornly.

'Then let me assist,' he offered. 'I took a call from your step-cousin Jamie last week in William's study. This morning my son took another call from him. To me your step-cousin mentioned a—proposition. With Robert, he simply rang off when he discovered that you were marrying me today. Maybe if you are wise you will explain the proposition, and why this man is still so much a part of your life that my son calls him *uncle*!'

The sleeping cat had awoken. Melanie watched with increasing wariness as the long fingers slid away from his ankle and his shoulders began to tense. She lost every scrap of colour and spoke without thinking. 'Anyone would think you were jealous—'

He moved like lightning, catching hold of her nearest wrist and pulling her across the gap separating them. She landed with a thud against his shirt front; her silk skirt slithered up her thighs as he hauled her onto his lap. Her fingers clawed at his shoulders; her breath panted into his face. His eyes had turned silver; she had never seen them do that before.

'Start talking,' he gritted.

She trembled all over, but held onto this one promise she had made to herself. 'Jamie is not up for discussion between you and me.'

'He was your lover eight years ago. I will not be betrayed by you twice!'

She struggled against him. 'Let go of me. You're hurting!'

To her absolute surprise he set her free. She slithered onto the seat beside him, too shaken to notice the new expression in his eyes. 'I apologise,' he said curtly. 'I don't usually forget my own strength. Where did I hurt you?'

'My wrist.' She was rubbing it, though it didn't really hurt. It had been the fear that he was close to hurting her that had made her tell the white lie.

Careful fingers took the wrist from her; very gently he began stroking the pink area with the smooth pad of his thumb. It was a stupid thing to react so badly to, but her pulse suddenly went crazy. He felt it happen and the thumb-pad stilled; she released a strangled little sigh. The mood flipped from anger to electrified awareness so quickly that it threw her into a state of confusion.

But not him—not him. He simply accepted the change with a shrug and a grimace, then lifted the wrist to his mouth and stroked the pink area with his tongue.

'So we're back to the sex again.' It was a supposed to be a withering condemnation, but it didn't quite come out like that.

'Blame yourself,' Rafiq murmured, and in the next moment she was pulled back into his lap.

'Don't!' she protested.

'Scared?' he drawled. 'Because you know your defences will not hold through one small kiss? Or is your pulse beating so fast because you are afraid that I *won't* kiss you?'

'No.'

He tested that denial with devastating consequences: the moment her lips clung he removed his own and watched her stare at his mouth like a hungry woman. One of his hands began to stroke her silk-covered thigh, left provokingly exposed by her slippery skirt. She moved against him, breasts searching for contact with his chest, her hips pressing into the cradle of his pelvis where the thrust of his erection was making itself known.

'You don't play fair,' she groaned helplessly.

He just laughed low in his throat, then gave her back his mouth. It stayed this time, seducing with lazy dips of his tongue, while he undid the jacket buttons and removed it altogether. Beneath she wore a creamy white body. One light touch and he knew she was wearing no bra. 'Interesting,' he murmured as the hand began to follow the clinging outline of Lycra. When the waistband of her skirt stopped his progress he merely switched attention to the other hand and finished the journey via her thigh.

A single smooth slide between her thighs and he had released the tiny poppers that held the body in place.

'Oh,' she whimpered, when he discovered for himself how warm and moist she was. For the next few dizzying minutes she just hung on and let him work his seductive magic. She moved, she stretched, she curled herself around him, she moaned into his hungry mouth. He broke the kiss on a hiss of tension, caught her chin between his teeth and bit, then her throat, then her breasts, first one then the other, sucking at them through the Lycra. She clutched at his neck, his hair, the hair-roughened wrist attached to the tormenting hand. She begged, she pleaded, he growled something and came back to pester her mouth again at the precise moment she was threatening to topple headlong into the kind of orgasm that didn't belong in this situation.

'We can't do this here,' she whispered anxiously.

With a growl of impatience he pressed his body forward, taking hers with him as he reached for the in-car phone. A few husky words in Arabic and the car was sliding to a standstill. Ten seconds later, Melanie heard the thud of a car door and realised that the driver had left them alone.

Embarrassed heat flooded her cheeks. 'He will know what we're doing!'

He was way beyond the point of giving a care. His

mouth claimed hers again; his hands claimed her hips. 'Release me,' he commanded in a throat-hoarse murmur.

'I can't.'

'You can.' Capturing one of her hands, he pressed it against himself. He was trembling as badly as she was, and maybe it was those tremors that stopped any more protest. A minute later she was straddling him, her mouth devouring his hot mouth while her body slowly took him in. She had never felt so wickedly wanton, had never thought she could behave like this. She moved while he held her slender hips steady; she copied the movement with her tongue. His breathing was ragged; the car filled with the scent of heat from their bodies. As she began to rise towards the edge, her inner muscles closed so tightly around him that he had to stop kissing her to throw back his dark head and close his eyes.

Pleasure like this could never be repeated, she found herself thinking as his hands reached up to frame her face and black eyelashes lifted to capture her eyes. She drove; he let her. It was a powerful, powerful aphrodisiac. When she leapt she cried out. When he followed he pulled her face into his shoulder and held her there throughout the ragged, pulsing finish until the weakness of exhaustion made her feel boneless.

They did not speak. Not then—not later, when eventually he gently eased himself from her and set her down on the seat at his side. Clothes rustled as shaking fingers replaced them into some semblance of dignity. Melanie kept her head lowered so her hair hid her hot face. She could sense the gravity shrouding Rafiq.

Cool air hit the interior as he let down the window. A minute later the car was moving again. The window remained open, though, circulating the hot air of seduction out of the car.

They turned in through a pair of high gates and began driving down a lane between a tunnel of trees with gnarled naked branches reaching out to tangle across the gap.

The car stopped. Rafiq climbed out and came around to open her door for her. Still without daring to look at him, she arrived at his side like a cracked piece of porcelain, in danger of shattering if anyone so much as spoke.

She found herself standing in front of huge sandstone monolith with tall sash windows and an oak front door. Beyond caring what this place was, she followed Rafiq to the door, which he unlocked with a key then stepped to one side, as if to invite her to precede him. She took a single step—that was all—before he was lifting her up in his big arms.

'More tradition?' she mocked shrilly.

'For once in your life keep your mouth shut,' he grimly advised her, and stepped over the threshold with his bride. He kicked the door shut again.

She gained a vague impression of oak panelling and iron fretwork, but most of her attention was honed on his taut profile as he proceeded to carry her up a stairway that curved around a panelled wall. They walked through an archway and down a dark red-carpeted corridor, passing more oak doors on their way. When they arrived at the one he was aiming for he opened it, then walked inside.

The room was so dramatically Gothic in design that she half expected to find a headless ghost standing in one of the shadowy corners. A fire burned in the grate of a big fireplace and a tray laid for coffee waited on a low table set between two richly upholstered wine-coloured velvet chairs. But what dominated the room was the huge and heavy oak four-poster bed hung with more wine-red velvet and, of all things, a dark purple throw made of silk.

The scene for a bridal seduction was set right down to the last detail—right down to the two matching black silk robes that lay draped across the foot of the bed. Shame, she thought cynically that they had pre-empted the moment; it had certainly spoiled all of this.

Allowing her feet to slip to a thick purple carpet, Rafiq

then turned to close the door. 'Sit down—pour yourself a drink,' he invited.

She almost jumped when he spoke to her. She spun on her heel then wished she hadn't done it when she found herself looking at a man at war with himself. He was yanking his tie loose with impatient fingers; the frown on his face was a definite scowl. Heat bloomed in her cheeks; shame choked her lungs. Turning away, she felt the sting of tears in her eyes.

'I don't like what you do to me,' she breathed out painfully.

'You surprise me. I had not noticed,' he drawled.

It was derision of the crushing kind and the worst insult he could have offered her. Moving on legs that did not want to support her, Melanie went to the nearest chair and sank down.

He disappeared through a door near the bed and came back a few minutes later wearing only a long black robe. She glanced at the bed, saw that one robe was now missing. It was so glaringly obvious what he was intending to do next that she wished she had never been born.

But what made it worse was the low soft pulsing taking place between her thighs. She could still feel him there, hard and silken. She could still taste his kisses on her tongue. He took the other chair, saw she hadn't touched the coffee pot and leant forward to pour it himself.

Silently, he handed a cup to her. With lowered eyes she took it. 'Thank you,' she breathed.

He huffed out a laugh. It brought her wary gaze up to clash head-on with his harshly mocking expression. 'How can you manage to sound so prim when we both know that prim is the last thing that you are?' he threw at her.

It was like being kicked when she was already down on the floor. 'I don't know how you can sit there and speak to me like this when you only married me an hour ago,' she responded shakily.

'And was seduced by you half an hour later.'

'You started it!'

'You finished it!' he raked back. 'In the name of *Allah* I cannot believe I am even sitting here with you! You are poison to a man like me.'

'Oh.' She stood up. 'How dare you say that?'

'Your step-cousin says I can say what the hell I like to you.'

He looked hard and dark and dangerously foreign. His anger and contempt washed over her in waves. Senses that just should *not* respond to this man she was seeing stung her with their awful message.

'I n-need to use the bathroom.' She turned away dizzily.

'You need an escape.'

'I *hate* you!' she cried.

He launched to his feet. She dropped her cup and ran towards the door he had used a few minutes ago as a dark coffee stain seeped into her skirt. Slamming the door shut behind her, she expected to find herself standing in a bathroom and instead found her eyes flickering round a room full of clothes. Men's clothes, women's clothes—rails and rails of them. It took only a glance at a couple of dresses for her to realise that every female item in here was so new it still wore its label.

Bought for her? She couldn't be sure. Didn't even think she wanted to know. They were her size and that was all that she cared about, since she didn't have anything else to wear and she needed to get out of this stupid wedding outfit that made such a mockery of the word marriage—and which was impregnated with the scent of him!

With trembling fingers she stripped the suit from her body and had just removed the wretched Lycra body when the door opened. She spun, clutching that silly scrap of material to her. 'Get out!' she shrieked at him.

With his usual arrogance he ignored the instruction. Instead he tossed something at her. She had to drop the body to catch it. It was the black wrap that matched the one he was wearing. It felt like the final humiliation to have him stand there viewing her through cold opal eyes as she fumbled on the robe over her near nakedness and dragged the two pieces of black silk across her body, tightly knotted the belt.

'Tell me about Jamie,' he demanded remorselessly.

He just was not going to give up!

'Which version would you really like to hear, Rafiq?' she flashed at him. 'The one where I admit to going from your arms to his arms with no conscience? Or the one where I tell you just how fickle you were—how easy you were to dupe and how badly you let me down when you dared to believe I could play such calculating games?'

His dark face tightened, big shoulders flexing at her bitterly deriding tone. 'The truth,' he gritted. 'Just tell me the truth!'

The truth? She almost laughed, though she'd never felt less like laughing. She wasn't that sure that he could take the truth! Did she actually care any more whether his pride was up to weathering the blow she could deliver it?

No, she didn't, she realised. He had called her poison. Well, maybe it was time he discovered just how poisonous she could be. So she lifted her face and looked at him squarely.

'The truth is that you were set up,' she said. 'Uncle Thomas and Jamie always knew I would inherit from William. William actually paid my uncle money for my keep. Uncle Thomas was greedy; he wanted to get his hands on *all* of William's money. But the only way he could do that was if he kept it in the family. He encouraged a romance between Jamie and me. I refused to play. They didn't like it. Tensions in the house became pretty grim. I decided I needed to get away and started hiring myself out to the local gentry to earn some extra money so I could leave the farm. Which was how I came to meet you.' She released a short laugh which stung with mockery, for never in a hundred years would a woman like her normally have come into contact with a man like Rafiq. 'You swept me off my feet and into bed, even asked me to marry you.'

'And you saw your quick escape from drudgery?'

Her eyes widened on this darkly handsome, beautifully put together man who could harbour such a huge inferiority complex. 'If I'd known about William's money it would not have changed anything. Haven't you noticed yet that I don't have much use for the stuff?'

'Unless you want to give it away to your step-cousin.'

He was mixing the past up with the present. 'Do you want to hear the rest of this or not?' she demanded.

A muscle in his jaw clenched tightly. He gave a grim nod of his head. 'I said yes to your proposal,' she continued tightly. 'And was then left with the unhappy task of breaking the news to Uncle Thomas and Jamie. They saw their chance of getting their hands on William's money slipping away, so they decided to do something about it.'

'I saw you with him in your bedroom.' His dark eyes were glinting as if he could still see them there. 'You were standing in your bedroom window, locked in each other arms.'

'I was locked in *his* arms!' Melanie flashed out the distinction.

He didn't believe her. 'Brazen,' he gritted. 'You were kissing as if you couldn't get enough of each other!'

He was right; the kiss had been fevered. Jamie had been feverishly trying to seduce her while she had been trying to get away! 'I was young and a complete fool,' she admitted cynically. 'I actually believed that Jamie truly loved me. I was attempting to let him down gently because I believed I was hurting him!'

'In your bathrobe. It was gaping.' His eyes were black with accusation.

'It was not!' she denied, paused to think about that, then had to offer a small shrug. 'Maybe a little,' she conceded. 'Things were getting a little out of hand, and I—'

'A little?' he cut in. 'Do you believe *a little* should mean something here?'

The jeering tone of his voice straightened her backbone. She looked into his hard, condemning face and wanted to hit him! 'Well, you tell me what *you* think it means, Rafiq,' she challenged. 'Or don't I need to ask?' It was written on his face! 'Because you saw me locked in that embrace with Jamie you just had to believe that I must be enjoying it! Didn't it occur to you for one small second that I might not have had much choice in the matter?'

'So you were the victim?' His tone derided her.

'As much as you were,' she replied.

'I know your passions,' he countered gruffly.

Melanie released a hard laugh. 'I suppose I should have expected a man from your culture to think like that,' she murmured bitterly.

'Meaning?'

'Primitive!' she flashed at him. 'I let you make love to me so, in your primitive view, it therefore goes without saying that I would let any man do that same!'

'I never said that.'

'You don't need to say it when I see it written on your face every time you look at me,' she denounced. 'The day I let you into my bed I lost your respect.'

Her shrug said she no longer cared that she had. As she began to walk towards him, Rafiq stiffened in the doorway. He had never seen her look upon him with such open dislike. 'I was twenty years old,' she said as she reached him. 'I let you take something very special from me. It should have meant something to you, but it didn't or you could not have walked away.'

'Your own uncle stood beside me as I watched you with Jamie. He told me things I would have been a fool to—'

'He lied,' she stated with a cool, quiet simplicity, then brushed past him to go back into the bedroom. Rafiq turned to watch her walk across the room with her shoulders straight and her slender shape shimmering with contempt for him.

The coffee cup still lay on its side on the carpet, a dark stain seeping outwards from its rim. He stood watching as she stooped to pick up the cup then reach for a napkin to mop up the stain. The soft fall of her hair curled around her slender nape and caressed the edges of the black silk robe. He could see her profile, delicate and pure in its smooth lines, even while her lovely mouth still pursed with dislike. Something shifted inside him—not sexual this time, but more a shifting of other desires—a desire to drop his guard and let himself believe what he knew deep down inside was the damning truth.

Because if what she had told him was the truth then it damned him and not Melanie. Because she was right and he had been fickle, easy to dupe. Most damning of all, he had let her down in the worst way a man could let down the woman he professed to love.

Primitive. He almost laughed. For primitive hardly covered the way he had behaved—if she was telling him the truth. At home in Rahman women might not enjoy the same equal rights as their western counterparts, but they did have the right to defend themselves when accused of a crime. He had denied Melanie even this basic right.

And in so doing he had forfeited the love she'd used to feel for him—and seven years of his son's life. Which left him with what? he had to ask himself. A marriage filled with bitterness and resentment? A wife who would never be a real wife to him unless he could accept her truth and put the past behind him?

Patiently pressing the napkin into the coffee stain, Melanie could feel his silence with every pulse of her heartbeat. She could sense his battle with every frail breath that she took. He had a choice; they both knew it. He must believe her or not believe her. She had no proof she could pull like a rabbit from a magic hat.

There were words, of course—lots more words. Were they worth uttering?

'They knew what time you were coming to collect me that evening.' She gave the words a chance. 'By the time you pulled into the farmyard the whole scene had been set so perfectly that I didn't really stand a chance. When I was allowed to turn and see you standing there, you were already turning away. I caught the next train to London...'

She paused in what she was doing and let the next ugly scene play inside the privacy of her own head. By the way he moved over, to stand frowning out of the window, so did Rafiq, she suspected.

'When I arrived back at the farm Uncle Thomas and Jamie were having this big row and I heard enough to know how neatly we had been set up. Jamie admitted his part in it before I walked out of there for good. He felt guilt...' Because I was so distraught. She did not say it out loud.

'Where did you go?' He sounded husky.

'To stay with friends in Winchester,' she answered, her fingers pressing at the wet patch again. 'I managed to get a job there, working in a factory. But they laid me off when it became obvious that I was pregnant. So I came up to London to try you again...'

'Hassan told me you had been trying to contact me,' he inserted. 'I was at home in Rahman. I asked Hassan to meet with you but you had not left a contact number. He did attempt to find you but was unsuccessful...'

Sitting back on her heels, Melanie looked up at his tall dark shape standing by the deep purple curtains, and felt something painful slice across her chest. So his brother hadn't even told him he'd spoken to her.

Neat, she thought ruefully. Tidy and slick.

'He merely said that he had heard you were living with another man.'

Pressing her trembling lips together, she refused to say

anything. There was enough bitterness flying around this room without her adding his brother into the mix.

He moved, shifting his tense frame to look at her. 'What happened to Jamie?'

'He left home too, went up north. I didn't hear from him again until his father died.' She stood up; her fingers were sticky and covered in fine fibres from the carpet. 'He's married now, has two beautiful children and a lovely wife he adores. He works with her father on a farm in Cumbria and would have been perfectly content to live the rest of his life milking cows for a living if the recent foot-and-mouth epidemic hadn't devastated the herd.'

'So he came to you for help?'

'Financial help.' Melanie nodded. 'They want to go organic, but it takes time to clear the land of chemicals, disease and…whatever else.' She shrugged. 'They still have to live while they are achieving all this. Then they have to restock their herd. They want to specialise, so I am investing half a million pounds into their project.'

'With no real hope of any return,' Rafiq added, 'because you still care for him.'

'Of course I still care for him!' she cried. 'He was sorry for what he'd done. What use is there in bearing grudges? He is my only living relative besides Robbie!'

'Not a blood relative.'

'Does that matter? Who are you to criticise?'

'I have a father and a half-brother.'

'Would you turn your back on your brother's wife if she came to you for help?'

No, he wouldn't. She could see that in the sudden frown on his face.

'We have wandered from the subject,' he said tensely.

'I've finished with the subject,' she replied. 'You believed what your eyes told you, and as far as you were concerned I did not warrant a single word in my defence. I gave birth to your son and with William's help brought him up. When I thought it would be safe to do it I introduced you to your son, and ended up—here.' She glanced around the Gothic bedroom. 'Married to a man who can't even look at me without seeing a slut.'

'I do not think you are a slut.'

'Poison, then.'

He released a harsh sigh. 'I was angry when I said that.'

'So was I. But do you want to know something really funny, Rafiq?' She lifted cool gold eyes to him. 'I really thought that you cared about me. Right up until you placed this ring on my finger I thought that, deep inside, beneath the rock you would call a heart, you still cared enough to want to make a success out of this marriage. But now?' She turned away. 'I think we've both made a terrible mistake.'

He didn't protest it, which more or less said the rest for her. 'Where is the bathroom?' she asked, holding up her sticky fingers.

He turned to open a door she hadn't noticed on the other side of the four-poster bed. And with her expression as closed as she could make it she walked past him into a rather startlingly decadent oak-panelled room with a huge free-standing bath tub overhung by a big brass shower head and a purple silk curtain that would circle the whole thing when closed. The rest of the fittings were antique porcelain. She walked over to the pedestal-mounted washbasin, then stood grimacing at her fingers before reaching for the taps.

Another pair of hands beat her to it. She was suddenly surrounded by Rafiq. Her body stiffened, her mouth ran dry. Water gushed into white porcelain, swirling around its curving bowl before spiralling its way down the drain. He took her hands and began to gently wash them.

Move back, she wanted to say, but found she couldn't. It just wasn't fair that after everything they'd just said he could *still* affect her like this!

'Mistakes, even terrible mistakes, can be rectified. You proved this yourself when you came to tell me about the wonderful child we had made. If I made a similar terrible mistake eight years ago then you must, in all fairness, give me the opportunity to make it up to you.'

Grave words, reasonable words, words that pulsated with the promise of a different kind. 'I can do this for myself.' She tried to defer offering an answer.

'But when I do it you know there is more to the chore than a simple washing of hands.'

Oh, dear God, he was oh, so right. She closed her eyes and tried very hard to stop a sigh of pleasure from developing. But, as with everything else about this extraordinary man, whether it be with anger or hate or sensuality, he moved her so deeply she really did not stand a chance.

His mouth found the pulse just below her ear lobe and his thumbs gently circled her wet palms. She was lost and she knew it. On a helpless groan she turned to capture his ready mouth. It was, she supposed, already written that they would drown their problems in the long deep warmth of the kiss.

A telephone started ringing somewhere. No one answered it. Was there anyone else here? Melanie tried to ignore it, wanted to stay just where she was in this man's arms, with his kiss filling her up from the inside.

The telephone went on and on until, on a rasping sigh of impatience, he broke away, muttered a curse and an apology, then went to answer it. The nearest land-line extension was downstairs in the study. As he strode into that room Rafiq made a mental note to get some extra extensions put into the house.

He knew so little about its minor details, having only taken possession of it yesterday. He had wanted somewhere special to bring them while William's town house was being attended to. He had viewed many properties, but this house he had liked on sight—had seen Melanie and his son fitting into it with ease. The master bedroom up there had seemed the perfect place to take a bride on her wedding night. Though now he had pre-empted that idea by a few hours, he mused grimly, as he stretched across the big dark antique oak desk to lift up the telephone.

'This had better be good, Kadir,' he barked at the only person who knew this telephone number.

What Kadir had to say to him set him cursing. By the time he put down the phone he was different man. He strode up the stairs and back into the bedroom to find Melanie standing by the bed—waiting for him.

For a moment, a short sweet tantalising moment, he considered forgetting everything except what this beautiful woman and the bed were offering him. Then reality hit.

'Get dressed again,' he instructed grimly. 'We must leave immediately.

CHAPTER ELEVEN

'WHY—what's happened?' Melanie demanded. He could see from her eyes that she was already thinking of their son and conjuring up some terrible accident.

'No, not Robert.' He quickly squashed that anxiety, though the one threatening to strike at him was almost as bad. 'Kadir has just received a call from my father,' he explained.

'He's taken ill again?'

He gave a shake of his head. 'It is such a rare occurrence for my father to speak to anyone outside his family that on hearing his voice Kadir went to pieces and told him about you and Robert and our marriage today.'

'You mean, he didn't know?'

'No,' he answered. 'No one in my family knows,' he added as he walked towards the bathroom. 'Now my father is shocked and angry. We have to go to him.'

There was a strangled gasp he recognised as anger. 'What were you intending to do—keep Robbie and me a dark secret for the rest of our lives?'

He paused in his stride. 'I am not quite that ruthless,' he countered grimly. 'But our marriage and the fact that we have a seven-year-old son is something I preferred to tell my father to his face. It is—complicated.' That seemed to be the word to describe the situation.

Not for Melanie, it seemed. 'Explain complicated,' she commanded, following him as he moved on into the bathroom.

His mouth flattened. He did not want to say this! 'He knew about our relationship eight years ago and is therefore against you before he even sets his eyes on you.'

172

She did not say a word, but simply turned and walked away. In a mood that hung somewhere between fury and frustration, Rafiq closed the door, shrugged off his robe and stepped beneath the shower.

By the time they met up again Rafiq knew hostilities were back with a vengeance. They met on the landing. Melanie had clearly used another room to dress and was now wearing a suit from the selection he had bought for her. It was long and slinky, in a shade of rich moss-green that did wonderful things for her sparking eyes.

By the way she pursed her beautiful mouth as she ran her gaze over him he did not impress, he noted heavily. 'It is expected of me.' He felt compelled to defend the long white tunic, dark red top-robe and chequered *gut rah* which was covering his head.

It was only when she walked down the stairs without saying a word that he remembered another time she had seen him dressed like this: he had been throwing her out of his life. A silent curse rattled around inside him. Once again he considered leaving his father to wait while he seduced this woman of his into a sweeter temper.

But shocks were bad for his father's health. Rafiq would never forgive himself if the old sheikh took a turn for the worse while Rafiq was lost in the act of lovemaking.

As they stepped outside the car was waiting with its engine running. As soon as they were on their way he offered his mobile phone to Melanie. 'Ring your friend,' he said, 'and warn her that we are coming to collect Robert.'

Without comment she made the connection with Sophia's mobile phone. 'We have to go to Rahman,' she explained. 'Can you have Robbie ready to travel by the time we arrive to pick him up?'

Whatever her friend said to her, Melanie's expression was rueful. 'No. But you had better prepare him for a bit of a shock. His father has turned himself into an Arab, so

if he knows beforehand he might not find himself looking
at a total stranger.'

With that, she gave him back his phone.

'Was that necessary?' he asked.

She turned an icy stare on him. 'Yes,' she said.

He released a sigh. 'It was not my intention for this to
happen.'

'Keep your excuses,' she told him. 'And just so that you
know,' she added, 'I am coming with you only because I
have made that decision. Your father deserves to meet his
grandson. But let one person look upon him like a leper,
Rafiq, just one—!'

'And you will do what?' he questioned curiously.

'I am relying on Rahman's reputation for being a free
and equal society,' she said. 'If I don't like what we meet
there then Robbie and I are coming home to England.'

'With or without me?'

'Without.'

He sighed and said nothing more. For what could he say
other than to offer yet another apology? But he suspected
it would not be enough for a woman looking at her ruined
wedding day.

The rest of the journey was achieved in silence. The
meeting with his son did not take place with shock but
with awe. 'Will I have to dress like that?' Robbie asked
dubiously.

'Not unless you want to,' Rafiq answered smoothly,
while Sophia Elliot looked on in complete silence. No
mocking tilt to a sleek black eyebrow, no glowering frown
of disapproval.

They made their farewells and within the hour were
boarding the Al-Qadim private jet to Rahman.

Within the next hour, his son was fast asleep in one of
the cabins and Melanie was curled up on a soft cream
leather sofa, clearly unimpressed by her luxury surroundings.

Rafiq decided that he had taken enough of her cold

shoulder. Picking her up as she was, he sat himself down and placed her on his lap, then lifted up a hand to remove his headgear and toss it aside. 'There—is that better?' Dark eyes mockingly quizzed her. 'Can you bring yourself to look at me now?'

What he didn't expect from his bit of sarcasm were the tears that filled her lovely eyes.

'You're ashamed of me,' she said.

'No,' he denied.

'If I had let you do it you would have brought Robbie with you and left me behind in London.'

'No.' He denied that too.

'You ruined my wedding day.'

'I will make it up to you.'

'You—'

It was no use carrying this conversation any further. So he kissed her. Why not? She needed kissing. So he kissed her until the tears went away. And kissed her some more until she slowly relaxed into a quiet slumber on his lap. He waved away the attendants when they walked down the cabin, and did not bother to move her to a bed because...he liked to have her just where she was.

Which meant...what? he asked himself as the air miles flew by them.

Hell, he knew what it meant. He had known it for a long time. A week—eight years—it mattered little how long he had known it.

They came in to land at dawn, circling around the perimeter of a great modern city which glinted in the early-morning sun. From the jet they transferred to a small Cessna, drawing curious glances from dark-eyed Arabs as they moved from plane to plane.

Rafiq flew them himself, leaving Melanie and Robbie to drink in the dramatic landscape panning out beneath them, with its silver thread of a river winding through a lush valley surrounded by high, lurking dunes and miles of sand. It took only twenty minutes before they were landing again. A four-wheel drive waited to receive them. Rafiq placed himself behind the wheel of this, and began driving them over tarmac towards a sandstone fortress backed by the fertile oasis of Al-Qadim.

Melanie knew all of this because Robbie had maintained a running commentary throughout both the short flight and this short drive towards his father's home. The child's grasp of this part of his heritage was so intense that even Rafiq allowed himself a couple of grimaces as he listened to him. But other than grimaces he offered nothing; his expression was sombre, the harsh lines of his profile telling her that he was lost in grim places of his own.

A pair of thick wooden gates swung inwards as they approached them, then closed behind them as they passed through into a beautiful courtyard laid with tropical plants and sparkling fountains. They came to a stop in front of a rich blue dome suspended on sandstone pillars. Rafiq got out of the car and strode round to the other side to open the other door. In silence he offered Melanie his hand to assist her to alight. Robbie scrambled out of his own accord, then stood gazing about him with dark eyes that greedily drank in every detail they could.

Then his father was quietly calling him to heel, and the small boy came with his dark head still twisting in frowning curiosity. 'Are we going to live here now?' he asked.

'No, we will continue to live in London,' his father assured him. 'And come here to visit during the school holidays, if you like.'

Nodding his head in approval, Robbie cleared the small frown from his brow, and walked happily beside his father into a vast entrance hall with a beautiful lapis-blue and white domed ceiling and pale sand marble covering the floor.

The first person Melanie saw was Sheikh Hassan Al-Qadim, and her heart slithered to her stomach. Dressed like Rafiq, he was standing straight and still beside a beautiful creature with dark red hair and perfect porcelain skin.

She was quite heavily pregnant beneath the slender white tunic she was wearing.

Both of them fixed their eyes on Robbie. Both looked shocked, if not dismayed. Melanie's fingers twitched within Rafiq's. He glanced down at her and she glanced upwards, the anxiety in her eyes making his grim mouth flatten as he looked away again.

Sheikh Hassan was looking at her now. One glimpse at his expression and Melanie knew what he was going to say. Her heart leapt from her stomach to lodge in her throat. He took a step towards her. 'Miss Leggett,' he murmured deeply, 'I must beg—'

'Mrs Portreath,' she corrected, leaping on anything just to silence him. His dark eyes narrowed and sharpened. With a minuscule shake of her head she tried to relay a message to him.

'Al-Qadim,' Rafiq corrected both of them. 'We married yesterday as you no doubt know by now, Hassan.'

'Of course. Rafiq, if you had only explained why you wanted me to be in London I would have been there. You know that.' Sheikh Hassan begged his understanding, taking the diversion Rafiq had unwittingly offered to him.

But Melanie could see he was not happy about remaining silent over their last meeting. As the two brothers greeted with an embrace and words spoken in Arabic those dark eyes so like Rafiq's remained fixed upon her over his brother's shoulder. She looked away, found herself gazing at the other woman, who had witnessed the exchange and was now looking very concerned.

She stepped forward with a smile, though. 'Welcome to our family,' she greeted warmly, and surprised Melanie by brushing a kiss to each of her cheeks. 'My name is Leona and I am married to Rafiq's brother,' she explained. 'Our child is due in two months—just in case you did not like to ask me. And this…' she turned to smile at Robbie '…has to be the most handsome Al-Qadim of the three.'

It was all very light, very eager to please, but Melanie

could sense the other woman's tension and she could see it repeated in Sheikh Hassan. She could feel it pulsing in Rafiq. When she added her own tension into it all the vast hall almost sparked with it.

'My name is Robert Portreath,' Robbie corrected with a faintly puzzled frown. The business of names was going to take some explaining later, Melanie realised as she watched Leona Al-Qadim dip down to his level to offer Robbie her hand.

'Then, I am very pleased to meet you, Robert Portreath,' she said gravely.

'You're English?' he said.

'Like your mother.' She nodded.

'You have very pretty hair and eyes.'

'And that,' Leona murmured sagely as she straightened, 'is most definitely the Al-Qadim charm. Hello, Rafiq,' she added gently.

'My lady,' he returned with a sweeping bow that held Melanie transfixed in surprise—until she realised she was seeing some kind of in-joke being enacted here, because both pairs of eyes were warm with amusement.

Then Rafiq was introducing his son to Sheikh Hassan, who bent to shake Robbie's hand very formally. When he straightened his eyes made that fleeting contact with Melanie's again.

It was Robbie who broke this next moment of tension. 'Where is my new grandfather?' he wanted to know.

All pleasure—forced or otherwise—instantly dropped away from everyone. Rafiq looked to his brother; his brother gave a reply. 'He is in his rooms,' his said quietly. 'He knows you have arrived.'

'Is he still ill?'

'Ah,' Hassan grimaced. 'His health is just fine; it is his temper that is threatening to fail him.'

It was automatic for Melanie to reach for Robbie, protecting her son being her paramount need. Rafiq noted the gesture and his expression hardened. 'You used to be famed for your diplomacy, Hassan,' he drawled.

'My apologies.' Hassan offered Melanie the kind of half-bow she was used to receiving from him. 'I was referring to our father's impatience at us keeping him waiting.'

It was a slick recovery, but a lie nonetheless. Rafiq saw Melanie's giveaway expression, went to claim Robbie's hand, then slipped his other hand back around her waist. She looked up at him, eyes anxiously searching his for reassurance.

He tried to give it with a small smile. But with his brother and Leona watching them Melanie knew there was little more he could do. They began to walk down a wide corridor between pale blue walls on sand-coloured floors. No one spoke. Even Robbie had picked up on the tension and was quiet.

They entered a room that might have been William's study in a lot of ways, though it was bigger and lighter and many degrees warmer. In the middle of the room, reclining on a divan, lay an old man whose fragile state tugged at Melanie's heart. That he was seriously ill was obvious; that he was resigned to that illness was written in his face. He lifted himself as they came towards him, though, sliding his thin body up a high bank of pillows and fixing his eyes on Robbie.

Rafiq went down on one knee to embrace his father. The old man's fingers held Rafiq's face as they spoke in low and husky Arabic. What bowled Melanie over most was the wave of love she could feel coming from the two men. It filled the room, tripped her heartbeat, while she waited for them to remember she and Robbie were here. Then Rafiq was turning and beckoning to Robbie. Tears glazed her eyes as she watched her brave son step into the curve of his father's arm.

An arm settled across her own shoulders. It belonged to Leona Al-Qadim.

'This is your grandfather, Robert,' Rafiq was explaining.

'Does he speak English?' the boy whispered.

'Yes,' the old sheikh answered for himself. 'I speak
many languages. Come…will you take my hand?'

It was an old hand, a gnarled hand. Robbie placed his
own hand into it without hesitation and allowed himself to
be drawn towards the divan. As he did so he slipped free
from Rafiq's comforting arm and, without needing any
prompting, began to talk.

It was his way. Melanie knew that; Rafiq had come to
know it. 'William said that you've been sick. Are you doing to die like William? I like your room; it's nice. Can
you play chess? William played chess with me. Have you
read *all* of these books?'

The old sheikh answered each separate question. He fell
in love as they all watched. As the questions flowed so did
Robbie's small figure flow into a sitting position on the
divan, then he curled until he was almost on the old
sheikh's lap. He was used to old men; he had grown up
with one of the very best. To her son there was no fear in
age and wrinkles. Melanie had always been aware that
Robbie missed William, but she had not realised just how
much until she saw how naturally he had drawn close to
his grandfather.

Tears blanked out the old man's image. Rafiq was standing straight and still. Leona's fingers smoothed one of her
shoulders, and somewhere behind her she was aware of
Sheikh Hassan's silent observation.

'You have a beautiful son, Melanie,' Leona said softly.

The sound of her voice broke the loaded atmosphere.
The old sheikh lifted his eyes and looked directly at her.
'You denied us all.'

It was a quiet and level accusation, designed to make
its point without alarming her son. Rafiq stiffened his
body. Melanie didn't know what to say. The sheikh was
right: she had denied them. The guilt of that was going to
live with her for a long time.

'She did not,' a sober voice inserted. 'I am afraid it is I who must take the blame for that.'

Rafiq turned to stare at his brother. Leona's fingers pressed gently into Melanie's arm.

'I'm going to take Melanie away now,' she informed all of them. 'Robert, would you like to come?'

It was not the voice of choice; little boys recognised these things. He scrambled down from his grandfather's divan and obediently walked with the women from the room.

'Don't shake so,' Leona murmured softly. 'My father-in-law is a good man. He just doesn't know the truth.'

'Neither does Rafiq,' Melanie said. 'I didn't want him to.'

'It is the way with these Al-Qadim men that they do not live well with itchy consciences. Hassan was honour-bound to tell Rafiq what he had done eight years ago from the moment he recognised your name.'

Leona led them up a wide staircase lined with pale cedar doors set into deep stone arches. It was a beautiful suite of rooms, wide, light and airy, in the coolest shades of pale aquamarine and ivory, with fretwork doors flung open to a balcony and the soft morning breeze.

A tiny dark-haired creature appeared from an adjoining room. She smiled at Robbie and held out her hand to him. 'Would you like to come and explore?' she invited.

Robbie looked at his mother; his mother looked at Leona Al-Qadim. 'This is Nina,' she explained. 'She is a trained nanny. Robert, if you want to go with Nina, I promise you will have great fun.'

The boy went without any more encouragement. As he walked away Melanie could hear him throwing out questions again. 'Are there camels here? Will I be able to touch one? Has my daddy got one I can see?'

'His daddy must be very proud of him,' Leona said gently.

'He didn't mention him to any of you,' Melanie pointed

out, and walked over to the open windows to gaze out on the kind of view she'd only expected to see on the television screen.

'Rafiq is an—unusual man,' Leona answered. 'He is a brilliant mathematician, incredibly loyal to the few people he loves, but he is a law unto himself and always has been. And his private life is generally sacrosanct.'

'Serena Cordero didn't think so.'

'Ah, Serena Cordero should be eternally grateful to you that you came along when you did.' Leona smiled. 'From what I can glean out of Hassan, Rafiq cancelled the rolling cheque that supported her dance tour, and which she was so fond of; then a few days ago he reinstated it. Said bitterness warped the mind, or some such clever phrase. We suspect this change of heart happened because you were busy turning him inside out. Though you will have to ask the big man himself, because he won't tell us anything.'

'So you speculate.'

'Yes.' Leona admitted it. 'We feel we have to. We worry about him, you see.' She released a sigh. 'I know you might laugh at this, but beneath that big tough exterior Rafiq is vulnerable to hurt.'

But Melanie didn't laugh. She shifted restlessly.

'You would have to know about the circumstances of his birth to understand this, his childhood living here in this palace as very much the resented second son of the old sheikh,' Leona continued, unaware that she was confiding in one who already knew these things. 'He is proud—too proud sometimes—and wary about letting anyone get too close to him. But from what Hassan has told me he took one look at you eight years ago and fell in love so totally that when you—'

'Accuse me of betrayal and I will walk right out of here,' Melanie cut in.

'Take note of that,' another deeper voice advised. They turned together to find Rafiq standing in the open door. There was a smile on his lips but his eyes were narrowed, and though he was attempting to look at ease Melanie could sense the tension in him, the anger that they were standing here talking about him like this.

'You're cross,' Leona murmured. She knew him well, Melanie noted. 'I was only trying to help Melanie to understand why we—'

'Then let me help you to understand,' Rafiq smoothly cut in. 'My wife did not betray anyone. But your husband may require your help to convince him that he did not do something very similar.'

'You've upset him.' Leona sighed.

'I forgave him,' Rafiq returned.

'Well, that only makes it worse!' she cried. 'You know what he's like; he will prowl around now, seething with frustration!'

Rafiq offered her one of those bows. 'Then may I suggest to my lady that she goes and joins him as he prowls?'

He was dismissing her, even holding the door open at the ready. Melanie decided she did not understand these people as she watched Leona Al-Qadim stroll up to Rafiq, smile and kiss him on the cheek before she left the room.

'That wasn't very nice of you,' she remarked as he closed the door.

'Leona is beautiful, charming and an absolute delight to be around, but she knows I dislike people meddling with my life.' With that the red-chequered *gut rah* was dragged from his head and tossed aside. 'As for you...' He strode forward, sending her spine erect and at the ready. 'You lied to me.'

'I did not lie!' she denied.

'By omission you did.'

'If your brother had kept silent there would have been no reason for you to know!'

'That you came looking for me while heavily pregnant with my son? That you took the risk of yet more cruel rejection because you cared enough to try again? That you had to sit there listening to him scare you with the kind of scenario that would make any mother's blood go cold?'

'He loves you. He was protecting you. I understand that now.'

'You understand nothing,' he denounced. 'I asked him to check if you were all right. I trusted him to do that small thing for me!'

'I was all right.'

'Well, I wasn't!' he rasped. 'I was out there—' he flung a hand out towards the sand-dunes she could see rising above miles of lush fruit groves '—pining for you!'

Pining? Melanie blinked. He spun his back to her on a tight hiss of a sigh. 'When Hassan told me you wanted to see me I did not dare go to London in case I fell at your feet,' he went on. 'But I needed to know that you were okay. I *hoped* that by some miracle you were going to tell him some magical reason that would make everything okay. I sat out there…' the hand flicked again '…waiting like a fool for the call that would send me to London on the next plane. What I got was a call telling me he couldn't find you but he had heard that you were living with a man.'

'I'm sorry,' Melanie murmured. 'I didn't—'

'Don't touch me,' he grated.

For a moment she froze in dismay. Then with a sigh she did the opposite, and walked around in front of him so she could wrap him in her arms. His heart was pounding, the great chest trembling as he fought a battle with himself.

He had lost, she thought. He had lost the battle. His arms came around her. 'I don't know what I am supposed to say to you, Melanie,' he muttered. 'You make me realise what a fool I was eight years ago. You make me face the high price I paid for my own pompous pride. You make me see that I have been treating you without honour from the moment I met you, and have done it all from a superior stance that deserves nothing but your contempt.'

'I don't hold you in contempt,' she denied.

'Then you should.'

'Because you believed what you were carefully primed to see?'

'Your uncle said some wicked things about you that day,' he said heavily. 'He poured out his poison and I, like a fool, drank it down, when any other fool would have known you were not the person he was describing to me.'

'If it had been you in that window with another woman and your brother pouring poison into me, I would have believed,' she admitted.

'Hassan did poison you.'

'He frightened me off for your sake. And he did it out of love, not avarice. There is a difference.'

'A forgivable difference?'

'You forgave him,' she pointed out.

'I forgave *him*,' he agreed. But not himself, Melanie defined from his tone. 'Tell me what you want from this marriage, Melanie,' he demanded. 'Tell me what the hell I can do to put some of this right for you.'

Lifting her chin, she looked up at him, saw glinting black eyes and harshly etched angles burnished bronze by the morning sun. 'I would like you to make love to me without thinking that you only do it because you feel utterly compelled to,' she told him softly. 'I would like to lie in your arms afterwards and know that you really want me there. I would like to look into your eyes and see tenderness sometimes, not just anger or passion.'

'You want me to love you.' He smiled oddly.

'I want you to *care*,' she amended.

'Take the love,' he advised. 'For it has always been there.' He grimaced, then released a long sigh and framed her face with his hands. 'Eight years ago I fell in love with the scent of your skin as you leant over my shoulder. I fell in love with the heat that coloured your lovely cheeks whenever I caught you looking at me. I wanted every part of you, every minute of your time, every kiss, every smile…' He kissed her. It was so tender it brought tears to her eyes. 'If you want my heart on a platter, Melanie, you can have it,' he offered huskily. 'I could not forget you—did not want to forget you. It was a lonely—lonely state of mind.'

There was nothing she could find to say in answer to that. Instinct—only instinct could respond. Her arms lifted to his shoulders and she pressed her mouth to the warm brown skin at his throat. 'I love you, Rafiq,' she softly confided. 'But you have to believe it if this marriage is going to stand a chance.'

'I believe,' he murmured. 'How can I not believe when you are still here in my arms after everything I have put you through?'

But he didn't sound happy. On a small sigh she lifted her eyes and parted her lips to speak again—only he stopped her. 'No,' he denied. 'Don't say any more. It tears me apart when we talk about those things we cannot alter. Just answer me one last question. Can we put the past behind us and start again?'

'Of course we can.' She smiled at him.

The smile turned his heart over. The shine in her eyes warmed him right through. Lifting her up against him, he caught her mouth with his and refused to let it go as he walked with her across pale blue marble and through a door on the other side of the room. The door closed behind them; he released her mouth only long enough to lock it.

'What about Robbie?' the mother in her questioned. 'He might come looking for us.'

He was already carrying her across to a huge divan bed that stood on a raised dais. 'Not while he has my father waiting to pore over maps of Rahman with him,' Rafiq lazily replied. 'And this is the beginning of our honeymoon.'

'I quite liked the Gothic setting,' Melanie said as he laid her down on a sea of dark red satin.

'Next time,' he promised.

'Why? How many honeymoons are we going to have?'

'A lifetime of them.'

He wasn't joking. Two months later they were back in England, locked away inside their Gothic mansion. Melanie was lazing in the bath when Rafiq strode into the room and announced, 'Hassan and Leona are the proud parents of a baby boy. Both mother and child are very well.'

'Oh, do you think we should fly back?' Melanie suggested anxiously. 'It seems wrong for you and I to be enjoying ourselves here when we might be needed there.'

'No,' Rafiq replied adamantly. 'Our son is with his new best friend—my father, Hassan and Leona are in twelfth heaven with their own son, and you and I, my darling, are on our second honeymoon here while Ethan Hayes and his crazy wife make William's house fit to live in.'

'You really should have told me about that,' Melanie chided as he strode towards the tub. 'I had a right to be consulted before you dared to touch anything in my house.'

'But the house does not belong to you,' Rafiq informed her as he removed his clothes. 'William left it to our son— though you saw fit not to tell me that. So I asked Robert's permission to renovate. He was delighted to give it. Unlike you,' he mocked her, 'our son had the good sense to know the house was in danger of falling down.'

'It wasn't that bad!' Melanie protested. 'And I thought Robbie loved it exactly as it was!'

'No, he has better taste—as I do,' he added arrogantly, referring to his good taste in wives.

With that, he stepped into the tub and slid himself into the water at the opposite end from Melanie. A hand reached up to pull a cord, which drew the purple silk curtain around them.

Candlelight flickered from hidden places. Silhouettes moved and came together...

$ Saving Money $ Has Never Been This Easy!

Just fill out and send in this form from any October, November and December 2002 books and we will send you a coupon booklet worth a total savings of $20.00 off future purchases of Harlequin and Silhouette books in 2003.

Yes! It's that easy!

**I accept your incredible offer!
Please send me a coupon booklet:**

Name (PLEASE PRINT)

Address   Apt. #

City   State/Prov.   Zip/Postal Code

**In a typical month, how many
Harlequin and Silhouette novels do you read?**

❑ 0-2   ❑ 3+

097KJKDNC7   097KJKDNDP

Please send this form to:
In the U.S.: Harlequin Books, P.O. Box 9071, Buffalo, NY 14269-9071
In Canada: Harlequin Books, P.O. Box 609, Fort Erie, Ontario L2A 5X3

Allow 4-6 weeks for delivery. Limit one coupon booklet per household. Must be postmarked no later than January 15, 2003.

HARLEQUIN®
Makes any time special ®

Silhouette®
Where love comes alive™

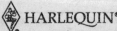

If you enjoyed what you just read,
then we've got an offer you can't resist!

Take 2 bestselling
love stories FREE!
Plus get a FREE surprise gift!

Clip this page and mail it to Harlequin Reader Service®

IN U.S.A.	IN CANADA
3010 Walden Ave.	P.O. Box 609
P.O. Box 1867	Fort Erie, Ontario
Buffalo, N.Y. 14240-1867	L2A 5X3

YES! Please send me 2 free Harlequin Presents® novels and my free surprise gift. After receiving them, if I don't wish to receive anymore, I can return the shipping statement marked cancel. If I don't cancel, I will receive 6 brand-new novels every month, before they're available in stores! In the U.S.A., bill me at the bargain price of $3.57 plus 25¢ shipping & handling per book and applicable sales tax, if any*. In Canada, bill me at the bargain price of $4.24 plus 25¢ shipping & handling per book and applicable taxes**. That's the complete price and a savings of at least 10% off the cover prices—what a great deal! I understand that accepting the 2 free books and gift places me under no obligation ever to buy any books. I can always return a shipment and cancel at any time. Even if I never buy another book from Harlequin, the 2 free books and gift are mine to keep forever.

106 HDN DNTZ
306 HDN DNT2

Name	(PLEASE PRINT)	
Address	Apt.#	
City	State/Prov.	Zip/Postal Code

* Terms and prices subject to change without notice. Sales tax applicable in N.Y.
** Canadian residents will be charged applicable provincial taxes and GST.
  All orders subject to approval. Offer limited to one per household and not valid to current Harlequin Presents® subscribers.
  ® are registered trademarks of Harlequin Enterprises Limited.

PRES02   ©2001 Harlequin Enterprises Limited

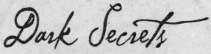

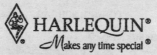

Harlequin is proud to have published
more than 75 novels by

Emma Darcy

Award-
winning Australian
author **Emma Darcy** is a
unique voice in Harlequin
Presents®. Her compelling, sexy,
intensely emotional novels have
gripped the imagination of readers
around the globe, and she's sold
nearly 60 million books
worldwide.

Praise for Emma Darcy:

"Emma Darcy delivers a spicy love story...a fiery conflict
and a hot sensuality."

"Emma Darcy creates a strong emotional premise
and a sizzling sensuality."

"Emma Darcy pulls no punches."

"With exciting scenes, vibrant characters and a layered story line,
Emma Darcy dishes up a spicy reading experience."

—*Romantic Times Magazine*

Look out for more thrilling stories by Emma Darcy,
coming soon in